Attack from Within

Book 2

Saving Superman Saga

Kathleen Sales

Attack from Within

2nd Edition

Copyright © 2014 Kathleen Sales

Author first rights

Word Count: 56,700

Cover by Al Esper

ISBN: 978-1-7352361-2-4 (sc)
ISBN: 978-1-7352361-3-1 (e)

Dedication

I dedicate *Attack from Within* to all my clients.

I enjoyed your company more than you'll ever know. Each of you taught me things I never learned in school. Thank you for helping me become a better doctor and a more compassionate human being. I hope my work, both then and now, improves your mental health and happiness.

Acknowledgements

The process of writing may be a solo flight, but it depends heavily upon the work of others. I want to thank Brian, my husband of forty plus years, for his support and critical reading of my drafts.

I owe many thanks to Cathy Kodra, a superb editor who worked overtime to improve both my books.

Other readers, including Joyce Leo, Dan Davis, and the unnamed veteran at Create Space who critiqued my draft, were generous in their praise and helpful with suggestions.

The impressive new cover was created by Al Unser. He not only designed the cover, he made all our interactions a positive experience.

I remain most grateful to you all.

Chapter 1

I waited in the lobby of a cheap motel on the poor man's side of San Diego, but it beat the heck out of anyplace I'd slept during the previous three years. I stared in confusion at my walking papers. No more uniforms, no guns, no bloody screaming bodies, no V-C with their booby-traps and mines. I was in the real world now, subject to civilian law, and I knew that would take some getting used to.

Key in hand, I found my room. Unlocking the door, I wrinkled up my nose at the reek of cigarette smoke, the wastebasket overflowing with crushed cans. Dumping my rucksack on the bed, I grabbed the phone, dialing long distance. The sound of her familiar voice made me grin.

"Hi Ma, I'm home—or at least in San Diego."

"Pete! You're back in the U.S.?"

"California. I'm due to catch a plane to Knoxville, through Atlanta, first thing tomorrow. I should land at sixteen hundred—sorry, four p.m."

"It's so good to hear you. How long can you stay?"

Obviously my discharge hadn't made their radar. I hesitated, unsure how to tell her. What could I say? I couldn't justify what I didn't understand.

"I'll be home for a couple weeks," I hedged.

"Your pa will meet you at the airport, and I'll call Sarah. Did you get my letter about her teaching license? I know she'll want to hear about the war."

I winced. The last thing I needed was to talk about the war. "Thanks Ma. Gotta run. See you soon." I slammed the receiver back into its cradle, knowing I should have told her the whole truth. She could have told Pa and saved me the trouble. I almost called her back, but I couldn't.

Coward. The word hissed inside my brain.

"Shut up," I whispered back. Seeking a buddy more attuned to my world, I pulled a card from my pocket and redialed. "Red?"

"Goddammit, Doc! Where are you?"

"San Diego."

"You're here? On a ship?"

"No, I'm headed home."

"Home? What happened? You get hurt?"

"Not really. Are you free?"

"Yeah, 'til five. I'm working evening shift. You wanna grab a beer?"

"Sure."

"Tell me where you are—I'll pick you up."

I sighed in relief and gave him my location. Right now I needed a good friend. While waiting, I pictured the short, carrot-headed ex-Marine. A sniper shot him in the knee four months back. I was there. While the rest of our squad focused fire on the sniper, I stopped Red's bleeding, stuck both an IV and morphine in his arm, and slipped an inflatable splint around his leg. He flew off in a chopper as our buddies dragged a bullet-riddled Charlie from the bush.

Red wrote me from the hospital, said I saved his life. That was a huge exaggeration, but his writing it still made me proud. He'd settled right here in San Diego—started school. In 'Nam he'd played the straight guy, always reliable, an effective problem solver, and the person you turned to when you had a FUBAR mess. I counted Red among a very few close friends.

Opening the door onto a concrete walkway, I felt the midday sun blast my face. But it wasn't steamy hot, not like 'Nam. Over there you could drown in your own sweat. Suddenly uncomfortable, I forced my attention onto a flashing neon sign, onto paint peeling off the cracked adobe. Nearby I heard the steady hum of traffic, the rumble of semis, the whine of police sirens, and smelled the scent of exhaust fumes in the air. This was America, my homeland, and in spite of the sirens, this city was far safer than the country I'd just left. Picking up my sketchpad, I found an empty page and settled on the steps, calming down.

A half-hour later a horn blared, and Red's baby-face appeared, smiling through the windshield of an antiquated Chevy. Closing the sketchpad, I jumped into his car. We grabbed each other.

"Hey, Doc!"

"Hey, Red! How's the leg?"

He shrugged, gently patting his left knee. "I can walk, and it doesn't hurt too bad. Guess that's the best you can expect. Anyway, I'm jazzed to be alive!" He grinned.

Driving on the freeway heading north, Red pulled off near the harbor, parking close to a dilapidated bar. Once inside, I grabbed a beer and found a quiet corner that offered a clear view of the room. Glancing around, I saw locals at the far side, a loner at the bar, and a Latina barmaid. Another door, probably to the kitchen, remained closed.

Red laughed, limping over to join me. "You'll get over that."

"What?"

"Casing for Charlie. You won't find him here."

I dropped my gaze, and he admitted, chuckling, "I still do it in places I don't know." Wincing, he settled his butt into a chair and gingerly straightened his bad knee. "You here to stay?"

I laid my papers on the table. He picked them up and frowned. "What is this crap?"

I shrugged. "Things changed. When I joined you guys, we were crushin' the V-C, but now they've turned the tables. On our last mission, we lost at least six men. Rog' is gone." I watched Red closely.

His eyes widened, and he grimaced as reality hit home. Then he sighed hard and shook his head. "You know what happened?"

"We were out on patrol and the V-C came at night. Rog' was on guard. Sometime around midnight, a series of explosions bounced me off the ground. I heard rifle fire—semi-automatics. I jumped up and grabbed my medic kit. Before I got far, I ran into Cole—spurtin' blood like a hydrant. I dug right in, closin' off the bleeder, but when I turned around, I saw an AK pointed at me. After that, I don't remember much."

Red's blue eyes narrowed with concern. "What'd they do?"

I shrugged. There was a gap in my memory you could drive a tank through. "The other squads moved in and cleaned house. They found lots of bodies, includin' Rog'. Then the chopper flew me to Da Nang. When my C.O. came, he asked a bunch of questions, but I couldn't remember what went down. They housed me in the brig overnight, but the next day they flew me to the Sanctuary ship. I worked there until I had a couple more blackouts. After that, they sent me home."

Red frowned. "Cripes, Doc. You were a great medic— saved a bunch of lives. You must have gone crazy for them to send you home."

I dropped my eyes, couldn't bear to meet his gaze, and eventually he looked away.

"Whatever shit happened in that hell-hole, I'm just glad you're here. When do you fly?"

"Tomorrow mornin'."

"I'd take you on the town tonight, but I gotta work. Soon as you get home, give me a call. Promise?" He waited for my answer.

I looked up and nodded, searching his eyes for the truth he wouldn't say. Red had put into words what I most feared. What was his opinion of me now?

* * *

The next morning I woke early and caught the first bus to the San Diego airport. The flight to Atlanta left on time, and I spent the next five hours staring out the window. Normally I loved to fly, but that day I felt trapped, stuck in a time warp like a dream where you're running hard but can't seem to move. I wasn't all that frightened, but I had a premonition that if nodded off, I'd wake up dead. Somewhere over the Rockies, I pulled out my sketchpad and examined the picture I'd begun at the motel. I started outlining Red inside his car and settled down.

The plane landed in Atlanta, a warm, soft shower dampening the tarmac, and I waited in the cabin with all the other civvies. Once inside, I stood behind the crowd, searching through departures for a puddle-jumper into Knoxville. I had two hours to wait and bought pizza and a paper, but when I didn't find any news about the war, I put the finishing touches on my sketch. Red's smiling face brought a smile to my own. At least one of my buddies had survived.

Before long I boarded my next flight, back to the valley and hills where I'd been raised. Change seeped slowly through those foothills, thinning into nothingness over mountain passes. Admittedly we had electric power and TV, were even working on a freeway, but our pioneer heritage of stubborn independence formed a thick, protective barrier across the Cumberlands.

I worried most about my pa. After everything he'd lived through, he would be the least forgiving of my discharge, and I'd grown up dodging his uncontrolled rage. Ma would support me, well aware of her own breakdowns. My sister Sarah, with her sharp wit and tongue, always saw reality more clearly than the others. She would, most likely, be okay. But Pa had his honor, an unbending moral code, and a Superman mythos to uphold. My general discharge would not set well with him.

Pa never met folks at the gate. I picked up my rucksack and went out to the entrance, waiting for him to bring the car. He'd traded in his Fairlane for a newer model Ford—a blue Falcon. About five minutes later, it cruised to a stop. He had aged since I'd been here, his brown eyes framed in wrinkles, his thinning brown hair streaked with gray. Is that how I'd look in another thirty years, except for lighter hair and blue eyes? Then he smiled, a rare occurrence, and greeted me with a formal handshake.

"Hi Pete. Great to see you."

I squeezed his hand. "You too, Pa. How you been?"

Not one to share his problems, Pa started up the car. "Let's go home and see what your ma is cookin' up." Putting the car in gear, he took the turn toward Knoxville.

"How's work?" I asked.

"Same old job, but it pays the bills. After you get out, you can join me, save on gas."

When hell freezes over. I should have told him I was already out, but I feared triggering him while he was driving.

"Your sister has a college degree now." Pa straightened up his shoulders with obvious pride, and I understood his need to brag. Aunt Kate had a teaching degree too, and she never failed to lord it over us. "When your enlistment's up, are you plannin' to stay in?"

I shrugged. "How's Mamaw?"

He snorted. "Same as ever. She's taken over Kate's house. Might be fun to watch the catfights, but it complicates life for your ma."

I puzzled over that. Back when I was ten, Mamaw lived with us, holding the pieces of our family together. She had a sense of fairness, of balance, that neither of my parents, nor my aunt, quite achieved. "How's Lee doin'?"

"Still in school and doin' fine. Always had more brains than brawn."

I nodded. Lee was half Chinese, very smart, and it pleased me to hear he was still in college. Maybe I should call him. He wasn't just book-smart, he also had more than his share of common sense. That was one reason I'd kept him as a buddy. I wasn't quite sure why he kept me.

After that we drove in silence all the way to Walnut Springs. I couldn't help smiling as the house came into view. Pa had painted it white since I'd been gone, and that day it stood out like a sculpture in marble against a forest background of iridescent green. As we pulled into the driveway, Ma came to the porch, as beautiful as ever with her long blond hair pulled back into a ponytail. She wiped her hands on the apron, and her happy smile crinkled to the corners of her brilliant blue eyes. I relaxed. There'd been a time when she couldn't bear to see me, but over the last ten years, we'd both changed—a lot.

Ma hugged me, but she stiffened, as if that encounter was a bit too personal. I released her. Shouldering my bag, I climbed upstairs. My room looked the same, except in miniature. The bedroom, house, and yard fit too tight, like a vise closing in on me until I couldn't breathe. I laid my discharge papers and sketchbook on the desk, stuck my clothes inside the dresser and trotted back downstairs.

"No uniform?" Ma said. "I want a picture."

I found a newspaper lying on the table, settled on the couch and hid my face behind the print. "I see they closed the coal mine in Kentucky." I glanced up at Ma. "Any news from Ricky?"

She wrinkled her forehead. "I think they sent him to prison for ten years."

I eyed the date—May 2, 1967. Ricky's pa died in that mine ten years back, and even though Lee's parents took Ricky in, he'd always found ways to get in trouble. His most recent fight sent him to Cumberland Mountain prison. I'd heard ugly stories all my life about that place—feared it'd be as dangerous as 'Nam.

Comparing my current situation to my friend's, I had to wonder if I'd done any better. Next month I'd turn twenty-one, and here I sat at home with no money, no career, no school, no job and a general discharge that suggested I'd gone nuts. I put the newspaper down and walked outside. The porch steps beckoned, and I settled there, relaxing in the late-afternoon sun.

Supper ready, Pa arrived and I followed him inside. Ma had gone all out preparing food: deep-fried chicken, baked potatoes, green beans, and her best homemade biscuits with real honey. We'd barely said grace when the front door slammed, and Sarah bounced into the kitchen.

"Hey, Pete. Welcome home!" She gave me a quick hug, blond hair in her face, blue-green eyes sparkling. "Meet Bailey, my boyfriend." She smiled up at a tall, preppy kid who'd followed her into the room. "Pete's visitin' us from Vietnam."

I stood up to shake Bailey's hand. He towered over me, although he lacked much muscle on his bones. He shook Pa's hand as well and nodded toward Ma, who was hurrying to put more plates and silverware around.

"Sit down and join us, we have plenty." Ma pointed to the empty chairs.

Sarah started loading up her plate. "We just came from a meetin' outside Nashville. Martin Luther King spoke, and this time he didn't draw a line at racial issues but openly came out against the war. Pete Seeger sang, and we raised a lot of money." She glanced over at me. "Time for all you sinners to come home."

I frowned, not because I completely disagreed, but because she had no right to comment on a war she had never seen, never fought.

"Oh, come on, Pete. You know I'm not callin' you a sinner. You're busy keepin' folks alive. That's great. But you shouldn't have to risk your life to do it. I worry about you!"

That made me smile. "No need to worry, Sis. I'm fine."

"What's your take on the war?" Bailey asked.

Shit! I had my back to the wall with unfriendly fire coming from two sides and a strong option for a third. I picked my words carefully. "It's a war. If you don't kill your enemy, you die. Those are your options."

Pa nodded at my comments and went back to his food, but Sarah wouldn't take the hint. "What if the war is wrong? What if there shouldn't be a war?"

"Soldiers don't make political decisions." I narrowed my eyes at her, warning her to quit, but even that maneuver didn't work.

"They could if they wanted. Just stop fightin'! If everybody quit, there wouldn't be a war."

I rolled my eyes and dug into the chicken. She sounded like a two-year-old screaming at a storm—a natural disaster nobody could stop. Silence ruled while we finished up the meal.

"Delicious!" I looked up and grinned at Ma. That was one fact we could agree on.

"Superb meal, Ma," Sarah said.

"Better than a restaurant," Bailey added.

Ma blushed with all the compliments and started gathering dishes. Sarah hurried to help while I made a rapid exit to the porch. Bailey followed, pulling out a cigarette. He offered me one, and I refused.

"How long's your leave?"

"Couple weeks." I winced at the lie, but I couldn't tell Bailey what I hadn't told Pa. *Coward.*

"You're a Navy corpsman?"

"Yep."

"You like the work?"

Wrinkling my nose against the cigarette smoke, I stopped to think. "Yeah, mostly. When I was on the ship, I enjoyed it, but out with the Marines…it got tough."

"You went out, like on patrol?"

"Yeah."

Bailey wrinkled up his forehead, staring worriedly at me. "You shoot anybody?"

I frowned. "I'm still alive."

He dropped his gaze, shaking his head in disapproval. "You're breakin' the Commandments. Why don't you become a conscientious objector?"

I focused on the oaks, so thick with yellow seedpods you could barely see the leaves. "Ah-choo! Sorry, allergies. I'd better go." I made a tactical retreat to my room and closed the door.

Chapter 2

The next morning, I woke early, my sleep cycle completely out of synch. Dawn found me at the creek, bamboo fishing pole in hand. I practiced playing the line across the water. That was no way to catch a catfish, but I didn't want to fish—I wanted an excuse to be alone.

This creek had been my favorite spot since childhood. Now early rays of sunlight dappled through the trees, highlighting the red clay bank, dark waters, rough gray rocks, and deadfalls of driftwood left over from spring flooding. Deeper in the water, shadows lurked, mostly catfish and turtles, but an elegant blue heron took up fishing at the first bend, and I could see his silhouette tall against the green—still as a statue 'til he struck.

Fishing brought back memories of Lee. I should call him. If he had the time and I could get a ride, maybe he'd meet me between classes. I needed to pick his brain, find some way to tell the truth without triggering Pa. With that thought in mind, I looked at the sun and realized the family would be up. I furled the line around my pole and jogged toward home.

I entered the kitchen to wash my hands, and the smell of eggs and bacon made me drool.

Turning from the stove, Ma studied me a minute. "Couldn't sleep?"

"Jet lag," I explained, slipping into a chair. "Scrambled eggs?"

She beat the eggs with milk, salt, and pepper, frying them into a savory yellow mash, which she dished onto a plate along with bacon. "Eat up."

"Thanks." I made short work of the food before I asked, "Do you know where Lee's stayin'—school or home?"

"I have his phone number at UT. You want it?"

"Yeah."

Ma rifled through her phone book and handed me his number. Dumping my dishes by the sink, I took her book to the telephone table. Overhead, I heard Pa tromping down the steps as I dialed and waited through the rings.

"Lee?"

"Pete! Where are you?"

"I'm home."

"Cool! You okay?"

The sudden tension in Lee's voice surprised me. "Yeah, I'm fine. What are your lunch plans for today?"

"I'm free from ten 'til two. Can you get here?"

I sighed, relieved that he wanted me to come. "I'll try. Where to?"

Lee paused. "Ayres Hall on the Hill is the easiest spot to find. If you ask anyone, they'll point the way. You hitchin'?"

"Yeah."

"Just be careful who you ride with. The truckers have takin' to beatin' up on students who can't pay."

I sniffed. After fighting the V-C, the thought of being mugged between here and Knoxville sounded silly. "I'll be fine."

"See you soon."

I returned to the kitchen and saw Pa chowing down. "Can you give me a lift into Oak Ridge?"

He looked up. "Where you goin'?"

"UT."

He glanced at his watch, gulped his coffee, and jumped up. "You ready?"

I ran upstairs for my wallet and met him at the car. He flew down the highway to Oak Ridge, stopping at a crossroads near a truck stop.

"If you need a ride home, call."

"Thanks." I waved, feeling guilty. I needed to explain about my discharge—soon. Maybe Lee could figure out a way.

The truck stop consisted of a couple gas pumps next to a dilapidated store/cafe. Inside, several truckers chatted at the counter. I chose a younger man seated alone. "You headin' into Knoxville?"

He looked up from his coffee. "Sorry, I'm scheduled to go to Chattanooga."

I nodded, eyeing the other men there, but they showed no interest in a hitcher. I wandered outside just as a black guy drove his old Ford pick-up to the pump. Walking over, I asked, "Where you headed?

"Knoxville." He cased me up and down. "Ya need a ride?"

"To UT. I'll pay a dollar toward your gas."

He grinned, took the cash, and paid his bill. Climbing into the cab, he opened the far door. "Hop in. You a student?"

I slid onto the vinyl seat. "Not yet. I just got home from Vietnam."

He nodded as he drove onto the highway. "My son's over there, fixin' trucks for the Army. He says the Viet-Cong are vicious, sneaky bastards—put explosives in the roads, in soda cans, even food."

"Yeah." I turned away, my mind picturing the outcome— the reduction of a human being into body parts. From the corner of my eye, I saw him glance at me and frown. He remained silent until we reached the freeway.

"Okay if I drop you off on Cumberland?"

"Sure."

He took me to the strip. I got out, eyeing the line of shops and restaurants and wondering where Lee would choose to eat.

"Good luck."

"Thanks." I turned and met his worried eyes. "I hope your son stays safe."

He sighed. "Me too."

As he drove off, I looked around. The business shops ran down the north side of the street. Across the way, the larger brick buildings dwarfed them. I had no idea which direction to go, so I stopped the first pretty girl I saw. "I'm new here. Can you point me towards Ayres Hall?"

She rolled her eyes and pointed down the street. Then with a disdainful flip of her blond hair, she marched off. I raised an eyebrow and followed, admiring her flowing hair and hips from a safe distance. A couple blocks farther, she pointed to a sign. I climbed the concrete steps to an elegant brick building overlooking Cumberland Avenue. Sitting on the steps, with my back against a concrete wall, I watched all the students come and go. They looked so young—straight out of high school.

I'd barely settled in when another guy stopped. He took in my buzzed head and walked over. "Been home long?"

I looked up, meeting friendly dark eyes above an easygoing smile.

"I'm Bruce," he said. "You just get back?"

"Am I that obvious?"

"Only if you've been there."

I remembered Red's comment on my checking people out and realized I'd provided all the clues.

"Pete." I reached over, shaking hands. "I just got home— meetin' an old friend."

"Where were you stationed?"

"Da Nang and Hue. Before that I served on the Sanctuary ship. I'm a corpsman."

He grinned and took a seat beside me. "They stuck me on a riverboat down in the Delta. You come through in one piece?"

"More or less."

He nodded, as if that remark made perfect sense.

"You?"

"I'm missin' a few parts." He held up his left hand with no fingers. "Grenade."

"Damn!" I studied the scars.

"At least this works." He tapped his head with the stump.

"You a student?" I watched his face, wondering if he felt as relaxed as his expression.

16

"Yeah, engineerin'. Takin' full advantage of the GI bill." He met my gaze, and I saw both curiosity and kindness in his eyes.

"School was never my strong suit."

"Well you can't be stupid, not and be a corpsman. Were you any good at it?"

I nodded. "Yeah. I liked it. What'd you do?"

"Fixed engines, drove the boat, kept it runnin'."

I nodded approvingly. Good maintenance prevented many deaths.

He glanced all around and lowered his voice. "Piece of advice, for what it's worth. Whatever happened over there happened in another world, or maybe in a nightmare. Leave it behind if you can. It won't help—can even hurt you over here. Gotta run, but welcome home and hope to see you around."

"Thanks." I watched him walk away, puzzled by his visit and advice. Jake had always encouraged me to talk, but that was ten years back and maybe things had changed. If he were still alive, would he agree? Maybe my life would go more smoothly if I just shut my mouth and pretended I was fine.

The clock hands neared eleven before Lee appeared. He was as short and slight as ever, dark eyes as perceptive, smile as engaging. "Hey, Pete. Need some food?" He jabbed me in the shoulder, snorted, and rubbed his hand. "You're like granite, man. Been working out?"

"If sixty-pound backpacks and thirty miles a day is workin' out."

"Whoa!" Lee sat down, studying me with a serious gaze. "Tough, huh?"

I nodded. "But I'm home."

"To stay?"

"Yeah, although no one but you knows it."

"Why not?"

I almost laughed. He'd cut to the crux of my problem in two minutes. That was so typical of Lee. "They sent me home early—general discharge—pretty much ordered me to go."

Lee frowned. "I thought you were a medic."

"I was, until a few weeks back." I glanced up at Lee. He'd put on his thinking face, paying close attention. I took a deep breath and forged ahead. "We were on patrol, camped for the night, when the Viet-Cong attacked. They killed the guys on watch and lobbed explosives where we slept. Somehow I survived and tried to help an injured buddy. I can't remember all that happened, but I know it was ugly, and we lost a lot of men. After that my C.O. sent me to the ship. When I couldn't do the work, they sent me home."

I glanced at Lee, but his face remained calm, as if I'd just described a fishing trip.

"It's the same as what happened years ago." He pursed his lips. "You couldn't tell me shit until Jake helped."

I thought back and realized Lee was right. I'd seen a man tortured and shot, my mother raped, while another guy put a gun to my head, molested me, and busted out my eardrum. But it'd taken a year to remember all that, and it came out hard, like shitting glass. Just thinking about it made me wince.

"It's how you handle stuff." Lee shrugged. "If you remember more and want to talk, I'll listen." He reached out and touched my arm.

18

I drew back, taking a deep breath.

"Let's eat." Lee led the way down to the strip, picking a small deli with a well-worn counter and cracked red vinyl seats.

After a ham sandwich, my brain cleared. "My real problem now is explainin' things to Pa."

Lee sighed, still working on his food. "What does he know?"

"He thinks I'm home on leave."

Lee pursed his lips. "The longer you wait, the harder it'll be for him to hear."

"I know." I focused on Lee's face, but he went right back to eating.

"Just tell him tonight, when you get home," Lee mumbled through a mouthful of honey ham on rye.

I sighed, realizing he didn't understand. "What should I say?"

My tone made Lee look at me and frown. "You can't make up a story, Pete. That'd be suicidal. Tell the truth."

The word *coward* hissed inside again, and my eyes burned a hole into the floor.

Lee raised one eyebrow, his slanted eyes narrowing and peering into mine. "What's wrong, Pete? You really think he'd hit you?"

I nodded, seriously considering that scene. "And if he tries, it could get ugly."

"Would it help to have somebody there?"

"Maybe, but I wouldn't want you gettin' in the middle."

"No way!" He rolled his eyes. "Tell you what. I'll drive you home and stick around for supper. When your pa's all relaxed, you can tell him."

"I don't want you missin' classes."

Lee pinned me with his no-nonsense stare. "You plan to lie? To him?"

I didn't need Lee calling me a coward. Leaping to my feet, muscles bunched, I walked away. Lee let me go, but I felt his eyes following as I left the counter and trotted down the street. After a block, I'd calmed enough to turn around. Seeing him waiting by the deli, I walked back.

"You ready?" Lee's voice sounded calm.

Envying his composure, I nodded. He led the way across campus to a crowded parking lot and unlocked a green VW bug. I climbed inside. As Lee followed the traffic headed west, I started to relax and look around. I hadn't been to Knoxville in years, but I was pretty certain the buildings here were new. "It's growin' fast."

"Yeah. They call this new area Cedar Bluff. No cedars and no bluff, but it's growing."

I chuckled. We had a standing joke about Walnut Springs. Maybe back in history, but not in my lifetime, could you find walnut trees or springs.

As we cruised up the highway, Lee asked. "How's your Pa?"

I shrugged. "He's okay, much as ever."

"If you could remember more, it'd help. He went through enough in World War II that he might get it. The gap in your memory makes it sound like you cracked up."

I glared.

Lee's eyes softened. "I know you, Pete. There's a good explanation in there somewhere."

We reached home around three. Ma met us on the porch, greeting Lee like a long-lost son. I loved that side of Ma. She never learned the meaning of the word "prejudiced." Lee and I snatched sodas from the kitchen and headed down our trail through the woods. As we passed the barn, I grabbed a couple fishing poles—mostly for show. At the creek, we found our favorite rocks and stretched out lazily in the dappled sunlight. Dropping lines into the water, we stayed quiet for some time until I asked, "How's school?"

Lee turned his head and smiled. "Love it. If I had the money, I'd stay a student all my life."

"What's your major?"

He grinned. "I've tried several: math, psychology, pre-law. Guess I'll stick with pre-law. Might become a lawyer. That opens up a lot of other options."

"Cool!" I could picture Lee in a business suit and tie or even in judge's robes someday. "You'll make a super lawyer."

"You think so?" His eyes sought mine.

"Yeah, really." I smiled. "You're smart and fair and levelheaded. I think it's an excellent fit."

"You want to go to college? Didn't Jake leave you money?"

"Enough to pay tuition for a couple years."

"What would you take?"

I shrugged. "I never much liked school."

"You never were that interested, but when you chose to learn, you did fine—like the project you finished on homeless veterans. Remember?"

I thought back. "But that was personal."

"So pick a major that's personal. What do you love?"

My sinker moved. I jerked up and hauled in a medium-sized catfish. "Fishin'." I unhooked my catch and dropped it into a pail.

"Be serious."

"I am serious." I poked him, but when he didn't smile, I dropped my head. "I liked bein' a corpsman. Guess I fucked that up."

"Maybe. Don't damn yourself until you know what happened." Lee narrowed his eyes. "That's like ruling on a case before you've heard it."

"Pa won't see it your way," I growled back.

"Yeah, I know."

Chapter 3

The sun had slid into the western sky by the time Lee and I hiked to the house. I cleaned the fish, Lee wrapped them for the freezer, and we washed up in the kitchen sink. Ma was busy with supper, so Lee and I settled on the living room couch.

Compared to Lee's home, ours was old-fashioned with two overstuffed chairs, a broken-down sofa, and a braided rug covering the old hardwood floor. There were no drapes or shades in the windows, which faced west, and the brilliant sunlight forced me to turn my head. I didn't see Sarah and Bailey arrive until they opened the front door.

Lee stood up and shook her hand. "Congratulations, Sarah! You'll make a great teacher."

Sarah grinned. "Thanks, Lee."

"He's majorin' in pre-law," I said.

Her eyebrows rose. "Impressive, but if anyone can master law, it's Lee."

"What's your major?" Lee asked Bailey.

"Paleontology."

I drew a total blank, and even Lee looked puzzled. "A study of prehistoric times?" he guessed.

Bailey's lanky body hunched over Lee. "Study of fossils. The real question is why." He glanced at Lee and me, but we were stumped.

"It's all about oil," Bailey said. "Energy! Certain fossils co-exist with oil. So where you find those fossils, you find black gold. It's a huge business, and they'll pay you big bucks if you're willin' to go scoutin' for deposits."

"Like off Vietnam," Sarah added. "A few years back, they found oil off the coast. Some people think that's why we're there."

My eyebrows rose. "Oil? In 'Nam?"

"Bet the Navy never told you that!" She smirked. "Most wars are fought over natural resources, like land, food, energy, and water."

"What about politics?" I asked.

She shook her head. "That's just a cover, along with all the talk about ideologies. It's all greed. That's why we shouldn't be there."

Bailey took a seat, smiling up at Sarah, obviously supportive of her views. Lee squinted out the window. "Your pa's home." I turned quickly as Pa came in the door. Lee caught my gaze and made a hands-down sign. I nodded back.

All through dinner, Sarah pushed her topic. She'd always been certain she was right, and now she was busily joisting against war, specifically the one in Vietnam. I wondered what she'd say if she'd actually been there, and it grew harder and harder for me to keep my cool. Pa focused on his food, but I could see the creases deepening in his forehead. Not wanting him to blow, I spoke first.

"That's rubbish! There's a civil war in Vietnam, north versus south, like we had a hundred years ago. Brother fightin' brother, and you never know for sure which side they're on. No one over there is talkin' peace, love, and charity. Even the children blow you up."

That brought silence to the table. Ma and Sarah rose to clear away the dishes, and Ma filled her glass bowls with homemade ice cream and fresh berries, which settled the argument—for now. After supper, Sarah and Bailey said goodbye and headed back to Knoxville. Ma started washing dishes, and Pa found his favorite chair. Lee nodded as I cleared my throat.

"Pa?"

He lifted his head and looked at me.

"There's somethin' I need to say."

He put down his paper and looked me in the eye.

"I've been discharged from the Navy."

Pa frowned as if he'd heard me wrong. "Discharged? Your enlistment ain't up." He tilted his head, forehead wrinkling as he thought it through. "What happened?"

I met Lee's gaze, and his look encouraged me, but I still feared Pa's reaction and kept my description brief. "They said I did a good job as a corpsman, but I couldn't be in the Navy anymore."

Pa stared at me. "You get court-martialed?"

"No! We were out on patrol when the V-C came at night, took out a large part of my squad. I was tryin' to save a buddy... when they caught us." I paused, unable to explain what I still could not recall.

25

Pa looked down, as if trying to digest the information. So far he'd taken it better than I'd feared, but now I saw him frown. "If they killed most of your squad, why not you?"

I shrugged. "Maybe 'cause I didn't have my gun."

"You weren't armed?" His eyes widened in shock and disbelief.

I felt my chest tighten. "I laid my rifle by my feet so I could close off a bleeder. Didn't have an extra hand."

"You're a fightin' man first." Pa glared at me.

"I tried to save a life."

"And killed the others? You shoulda dropped that stuff and shot the bastards!" His face distorted into an angry mask. "You can't play Boy Scout in the middle of a war. No wonder they discharged you—you let your buddies die!" He sprang to his feet, eyes glazing over as he screamed, "You're such a coward!"

Furious, I stood facing Pa. We glowered at each other, nose to nose, fists clenched. Lee spoke, but I couldn't hear his words. I wanted Pa to hit me first, give me an excuse to level him.

His strong left hook smashed my nose. I yelped, pain doubling me in half. Quicker than a snake, I sunk my fist below his belt. He went to his knees, gasping for breath.

I stepped back, appalled at what I'd done but still so pissed I nearly kicked him. Ma came running to his side as I escaped onto the porch. I collapsed there, hands covering my nose.

Lee followed. Closing the front door, he stared down at my blood-covered hands. "Did he break it?"

"I think so."

"I'll drive you to the ER."

Standing, I felt woozy and grabbed at the rail. Regaining my balance, I followed slowly to Lee's car. As he drove to the highway, putting distance between Pa and me, I relaxed.

"Is Pa okay?"

Lee shrugged. "Your ma's with him."

At the Harriman hospital, they rushed me to the ER while the nurse called their doctor at his home. A few minutes later, she introduced a large man with a mane of graying hair. Assessing the damage with his flashlight, he nodded. "Yep, it's broke." He placed both his hands against my face, thumbs on my nose. "Best thing to do is set it straight. Hang on."

I grabbed the table but yelped loudly when he snapped the bone back into place.

"All done." He examined his handiwork with pride while the nurse gently washed my nose and face before taping a splint across the bone. "I'll pack it now, stop the bleeding," He used a hemostat to stuff gauze up my nose. "You'll have to breathe through your mouth the next few days. She'll give you an appointment, and when you come back, I'll remove the packing and make sure you're healing up. Don't be surprised if your nose swells a bit and you develop bruising. Ice will help."

I paid my bill, a sizeable bite out of my severance pay, and picked up a prescription of pain pills. Back in the car, Lee asked, "Where to?" That stopped me. I couldn't go home and glanced hopefully at Lee.

"You want to sleep at my place?"

I nodded, and Lee drove us back toward Knoxville. "You got plans?" he asked as we traveled down the highway.

"Find a job."

"School?"

I shook my head. There was nothing pushing me in that direction. We rode silently through a sea of headlights, stopping outside a multistory brick building. Lee led the way up several flights of stairs and into a small studio apartment. I sank into the nearest chair while he brought water for my pill.

"Let me know if you need anything else. I have to study," he explained, pulling out a pile of books.

Silence suited me well—I had nothing left to say. The chair faced a window, and I gazed out at the city with its Christmas tree buildings, their windows all alight. Car headlights flashed past like a swarm of fireflies. But as I peered inward toward the darkness of my past, the world outside just disappeared. Lost in memories of home, memories of 'Nam, I saw no lights leading to my future.

That night Lee piled up blankets on the floor, but even with the pain pill, I couldn't get to sleep. What would I do? I'd enjoyed working as a corpsman and wanted to go back, wanted to stay there on the ship. Why hadn't I argued? Why hadn't they explained what I'd done wrong? I punched the pillow, remembering other times I'd fought with Pa. He'd first whipped me when I wasn't yet eleven, but I'd made it all the way to Nashville.

Of course I was trying to find Jake. He'd promised to take me on trips around the world, and he wouldn't let a fistfight slow him down. As I pictured Jake's bearded face and crinkly blue eyes, my mind cleared. I needed to go home and pack my rucksack. I needed my map and the bankbook Jake had sent. Then I would leave—this time for good.

How would I travel? Jake had taught me to ride freights, but over the last ten years, the rules had tightened up. I'd need a car. That would take a big part of his savings, but with a car, I could drive anywhere I chose. For the first time that day, I felt relief. Having reached that decision, I took another pill and finally slept.

Lee woke me the next morning. "You okay?"

"Yeah," I mumbled.

"I've gotta run. After my class, I'll take you home to get your stuff."

With effort, I opened up my eyes and saw Lee, dressed for school and frowning down at me.

"Go back to sleep," he said. "Or if you're hungry, raid the fridge. Just don't look in the mirror, and don't leave. Promise?"

I grunted, closed my eyes, and fell asleep. Lee woke me again when he returned. That time I managed to sit, leaning up against the bed. He brought me coffee, which I sipped, gradually recalling what he'd told me earlier.

"I look that bad?"

"You're a real head-turner, my friend. Can you get up?"

I stumbled to my feet and made it to the toilet. Back in the living room, I collapsed into a chair. Lee brought me Pop-Tarts, which I nibbled. My head throbbed, and the simple act of chewing made it worse. But as I stayed upright, the intensity eased off.

Lee narrowed his eyes. "How about I go and get your things. What do you need?"

I would have objected but doubted I could climb stairs or carry anything "My bag's beneath the bed. Stuff everythin' inside the dresser in it, take the map off the wall, fold it up, and get Jake's bankbook from the top dresser drawer. Oh yeah, my papers and sketchbook are sittin' on the desk. Bring them too."

"You got a coat, hat, gloves?"

"Downstairs in the closet. And grab my bamboo pole, if you have time."

"No problem," Lee said. "Your pa will be at work. You need another pain pill?"

I shook my head very carefully. Lee nodded and took off. As soon as he left, I stumbled back into the bathroom and stared at the mirror. My eyes had swollen almost shut, the lids turning purple, and the bruising extended to my lip. I couldn't see my nose but imagined it looked worse. Not trusting myself to stay upright in the shower, I swallowed another pain pill and slept sitting in the chair.

Lee nursed me for three days before I went to see the doctor. When he pulled out the packing, it hurt, but with the gauze gone, I could breathe and that felt great. The doc said to keep the splint on for at least six more weeks. I nodded, paid my bill, and left.

After the appointment, Lee drove me into Knoxville, to the Bank of America downtown. I pulled out Jake's savings book and asked the pretty teller to withdraw all my funds. She took my ID and disappeared.

When she returned, she shook her head. "This was deposited in our Alaska branch, and they won't open until mid-afternoon. Check with me then."

Lee drove us to UT, and he was right—just walking across campus, I turned heads. Over lunch Lee asked, "What you plannin' to do with all that money?"

"Buy a car."

He raised his eyebrows. "You leaving?"

I nodded, munching slowly on my pizza. "I'm gonna drive around the country, startin' with Detroit."

"Detroit? The murder city?" His eyes narrowed into slits.

"They have jobs."

Lee shook his head. "That's like another war zone, Pete. You don't need that now. Why don't you stay with me and use Jake's money for tuition?"

"Maybe later. Not today."

Lee's eyes fixed on mine. "I've been reading up on battle stress. They say there's a tendency to repeat the trauma, maybe as a way of mastering the past, but it leads survivors into danger— like Detroit. You could visit the VA and talk to a counselor. Even your friend, Jake, saw a shrink."

Coward! As that word hissed in my mind, my fists grew tight beneath the table. Taking a deep breath, I shook my head. "I have to get far away from Pa. I can't stay here."

Lee didn't argue. We drove back to the bank, and they took another hour clearing up the details. Finally they counted out my cash—a thousand dollars plus! I'd never held that much money in my life. I stuck the bills into my wallet as Lee drove down Kingston Pike, stopping at the first car lot we saw. Under other circumstances, I'd have asked Pa for help. Neither Lee nor I was a mechanic.

A red VW Beetle caught my eye, and I walked around it, examining the paint. There were a few scratches but no dents.

"That car is a fantastic deal." The salesman smiled wide. "Only fifty thousand miles, good tires, new clutch, and great gas mileage, for a mere five hundred ninety bucks."

"Does it burn oil?"

In answer he pulled a key off his ring, unlocked the door, and started up the car. It purred happily with not a hint of smoke, but I knew there were many ways to cover up that fault and asked to take it for a spin. He agreed, provided that Lee leave his car behind.

I drove the red VW out onto the highway, pushing up the speed while testing the brakes and steering. Next I stopped and let it cool, starting it again—still no smoke. I climbed underneath, looked for oil, and checked for water leaks in the radiator and hoses. Every part of the engine appeared clean.

I drove back to Lee's apartment and gathered my belongings, packing them inside the hood. Back at the car lot, I haggled the salesman down to five hundred even. The license and title would be sent to Lee's apartment. Once I'd taped the temporary license in the window, I grabbed hold of Lee's hands.

"Stay out of trouble, buddy," Lee said, his dark eyes staring worriedly at me.

"I will, and many thanks. Ace your test today, and I'll talk with you real soon."

Back at Lee's apartment, I picked up all my gear and then drove my car to Walnut Springs. Ma wasn't home. I sat gazing at the house and barn and finally chose to walk down to the creek. It was drizzling, but I didn't care.

Standing by the water brought back memories: Lee and me sliding off the rocks into the creek, Pa teaching us to fish, Jake and I talking about my time in Memphis, and me praying hard after his death. Sadness washed over me as I prayed again, asking Lord Jesus for his guidance.

Calmer, I walked back to the house and saw Ma's car. She was bringing in the groceries, so I helped. Back in the kitchen I said, "I bought a car."

She nodded, having seen it, and looked up. "Are you okay?"

I realized she was staring at my nose. "I'll be fine."

"You leaving?"

I nodded.

"Where to?"

"I'm headed north. There are lots of jobs up in Michigan. I'll hang out there for the summer, maybe come back in the fall."

"Where will you live?"

"I'll let you know." I leaned down and kissed her on the cheek.

She rechecked the grocery list, hiding her tears. Eventually she raised her eyes to mine. "You know your pa's not really a bad person."

"Yeah I know, but he needs time to think things through. So do I. It will work out better if I leave."

Ma nodded, finishing up her groceries. "Can you stay for supper?"

I tried to raise an eyebrow, but that hurt. "You know I love you, Ma, and when the time is right, please tell Pa I love him too."

Chapter 4

The second day on the road, I reached inside my rucksack and discovered a slightly used .45 revolver. I knew it had to come from Lee, and his concern for my safety made me smile. The previous night I'd crossed the Michigan state line and slept in my car at a turn-off near a cornfield. The land was flatter here, the soil richer than back home. I could work as a farmhand—Jake had taught me—or I could work in a factory in Detroit.

I suspected I'd make better money in Detroit, and I'd find more people, nightlife, and girls. That decided, I followed the freeway into town. I'd driven through other cities coming up—Cincinnati, Dayton, and Toledo were good sized—but none as massive as Detroit. The suburbs extended out thirty miles or more, and several major freeways crisscrossed through downtown, merging onto the bridge to Canada.

I bought a map and memorized the layout of Detroit. The center of the city faced south to the river. From that hub, the avenues fanned outward like spokes—a half-wheel crisscrossed with streets running east to west. "Eight Mile" marked the northern edge of Detroit proper, but the suburbs spread northward off the map.

Once I'd learned the major arteries, I bought two local papers and studied the ads. There were jobs, although the wages weren't that high. I'd probably need to join a union for good pay. First thing, I drove to River Rouge—the huge Ford plant, easily a mile on each side. I'd read they took iron ore off ships, processed it to steel, manufactured all the parts, and assembled them into finished cars—all at this plant. From miles down the road, I could see the giant smokestacks belching pollution into the air. In the neighborhoods nearby, black soot covered the parked cars, yards and pavement. I wondered if the factories were as filthy.

They'd hung a "HIRING" sign on the gate, so I drove through and parked, walking across the massive lot to the guardhouse.

"What ya want?" a black guard asked.

"A job."

"What ya do?"

"Most anythin'."

He shook his head. "They's only wantin' trained people, son. You could try GM, out on Clark Street."

"Thanks." I turned and walked away. Back in the car, I drove slowly across town. At the GM plant, they refused my application. I suspected I'd do better if my skin were three shades darker or I had a special skill. As I drove through the neighborhood bordering the plant, many of the houses appeared to be deserted, and others needed paint and repairs. On the main streets, half the storefronts stood abandoned. The people I saw— mostly black—looked hungry, angry and ready for a fight.

35

As I drove back to the farmlands, a heavy weight pressed down on my chest. I needed a job, but Detroit seemed so forbidding it made Y-12, where Pa worked behind high fences and barbwire, look like Eden.

Resting in my car, I read the ads more carefully. Experience clearly was the key. Anyone without it earned one buck an hour— minimum wage. My experience was in patching people up, but I didn't have the license or degrees required for the hospital jobs I saw. My eyes stopped when I found an ad for roofers. I'd helped Pa with roofing, painting and repairs. Going back through the ads once again, I made a list of work sites. Picking up a pizza loaded with pepperoni, I returned to my turn-off and curled up to sleep.

The next day, I visited all the building sites. New construction seemed cleaner and more cheerful than the plants, so I sold myself as an experienced roofer. Before long I was a dozen stories up, walking on beams to frame a roof. The sunshine and fresh air invigorated me, and I gratefully settled into work. I'd missed the Navy discipline more than I knew, and now the sound of voices, cursing and jokes put me in the mood to hum Ma's gospel music. My tunes plus my accent quickly earned me a nickname—Tennessee.

By the end of the day, I felt good, until I reached into my pocket and found my wallet missing. It held all my money, almost five hundred dollars. I scrambled down and searched the site, talked with all the workers, but my wallet had simply disappeared.

That happened on a Tuesday, and Friday was payday. That night I ate the remains of last-night's pizza, praying it hadn't spoiled in the heat. But it had. The next day at work, I ran to the outhouse more times than I could count.

"Hey, Tennessee," one of the workers yelled. "You call that dance the Tennessee waltz?"

By lunchtime, I felt whipped and ready to leave when a slightly older guy walked my way. I'd seen him around and the workers called him Vic. At first glance, he reminded me of Rog', tall and handsome with almond-colored skin, black kinky hair buzzed short, and hazel eyes. The resemblance triggered such a painful memory, I turned around and walked away.

Vic touched my shoulder and I pivoted quickly, ready for a fight.

"You need something?" he asked, his deep voice gentle.

"No thanks." My gut cramped at the very thought of food.

"I meant drugs for your waltz, not to mention your face. Were you in an accident?"

I shook my head, looking down.

He motioned me to follow and walked back to a car, opening the trunk. Inside, he searched through boxes filled with pills of various kinds and pulled out a bottle. He handed it to me. "Paregoric, tincture of opiate. It won't make you high, but it'll slow down your trots."

I hesitated, worried about cost.

"Just take it, Tennessee. Need some pain meds, food?"

"I can't eat."

He handed me a bottle of water and some crackers. "Once your gut settles, try these."

I accepted his gifts, drinking the medicine and waiting an hour before I dared to sample the rest. By late afternoon, I felt almost human. At quitting time, Vic walked me to my car.

He peered inside and saw the sleeping bag. "You need a room?"

"Same problem." I patted my flat pocket.

"Yeah, but you'll get paid. Come to my place for the night—see what you think."

I hesitated, but his lunchtime cocktail had set my system straight, so I trusted him as much as I trusted anyone. I trailed him down Woodward, and we turned onto a quiet street with trees and big houses lining either side. A few blocks farther, he pulled over to the curb. I followed suit.

The old house rose a sizeable three stories and included an inviting covered porch. The door was unlocked, and we walked into a large room with wooden floors. A dozen mismatched chairs surrounded a big table, and to my left a wide archway opened into a parlor—painted red. Bay windows draped with velvet curtains faced the street, and a fake Persian carpet softened the wood floor. The only piece of furniture was a dark-blue velvet sofa, but large cushions lay around in lieu of chairs.

A tiny, dark-haired girl came from the kitchen. "Hi, Vic." She gave him a quick kiss and turned toward me.

"Meet Tennessee." Vic winked in my direction. "This is Lou."

I shook her hand. "Lovely home."

"Oh, it's not mine, its Vic's. I pay rent, along with all the other roomies. If you stay for dinner, you can meet them," Lou explained.

As she spoke, the front door opened and a tall slender woman wearing a white uniform walked in. Her light-brown hair was long and silky, her eyes an unusual jade green.

"Hi Lou, Vic. Who's your friend?"

"I call him Tennessee, but that's not his real name." Vic raised an eyebrow at me.

"Pete Martin."

"Laura Davenport." She held out her hand. I took it in mine, enjoying the sensation, which made me hold on a bit too long. She pulled away and turned to Lou. "What's cooking?"

"Spaghetti, and I bought some garlic bread. You gonna make a salad?"

The girls retreated to the kitchen just as Vic came through the doorway, carrying two beers. He intentionally bumped into them and fondled Laura's ass along the way. She glared at him, fire in her eyes. Vic handed me a beer, and I relaxed on the couch while Vic leaned back against the wall.

"This is a communal house," he said. "We share everything: expenses, food, utilities, and maintenance. One of our roomies just got drafted, so right now we have a vacant room. You wanna see?"

I followed him up a long flight of stairs, admiring the handrail and oak trim. There was a bathroom at the top, and Vic entered the bedroom to its right. A big, soiled mattress lay on the wooden floor, and a cheap dresser leaned against the wall. The floor needed washing, but at least there was a window, which stood open.

"How much per month?"

"Thirty bucks, but you'll have to buy some groceries and help around the house."

"How's the neighborhood?"

He shrugged. "As good as you'll get inside Detroit. This area is known as the 'red-light district.'" He raised an eyebrow at my snort. "You don't have to sample, but cops patrol the streets. So it's pretty safe—even at night."

That made sense, and with my current wage of two dollars an hour, I could easily pay rent and buy some food. For the first time since my money disappeared, I relaxed.

Vic raised an eyebrow. "Don't decide yet. Wait 'til you meet the other roomies."

I cleaned up in the bathroom before following Vic downstairs. Several new people had gathered in the parlor. Vic introduced me to Phil and Ron, who occupied the suite above the parlor. Phil was tall and lean, like Vic but darker skinned with features more African than white, and I pegged Ron as an Italian. A red-haired teen named Anna occupied the attic, and a muscular woman with very short brown hair called herself Madge and claimed the room across from mine. That meant Vic and Lou had the room next to me, and Laura had the room at the far end.

I watched Phil and Ron flirting with each other, oblivious to my curious stare. When Vic glanced at me, I dropped my gaze. Observing their affection was both new and disconcerting. In the Navy, that kind of homosexual display would most likely lead to violence. Pa would throw them out on their ears

Lou announced supper, and we gathered at the table, passing food, chowing down, and telling stories. Madge talked about her books, both the boxes she stacked and packed and those she hoped to write. Ron and Phil discussed their day's drug sales with Vic. To my relief they didn't sell the hard stuff, just prescription drugs at wholesale prices and pot. Anna chatted shyly about far too many boyfriends. I guessed she might be a prostitute. Laura didn't talk about herself.

A strange collection of people, but they all seemed content, comfortable in their peculiar roles. No one ridiculed my accent, dirty clothes, or BO after working two days in the heat. I could find another room, but not 'til after I got paid. Anyway, I felt at home right here.

Watching Laura from the corner of my eye, I wondered what accident of life had led her to join this communal family. "Laura, where you from?"

"A farm up in the thumb." She used her hand as a map of Michigan and pointed to the middle of her thumb.

"Why'd you move here?"

"Nursing school."

I cocked my head, pretty certain there were nursing schools closer to her home. She gave no more hints about her past but started to talk about her work.

"I saw a kid today, broken arm. We x-rayed the other arm, just for comparison, and that showed a recently healed fracture. The doctor asked for X-rays of his legs, and both ankles had healed breaks. We called DHS and got permission to keep him— although they'll probably send him home."

"They can't do that!" Phil snarled. "The new law is supposed to protect abused kids."

"We can't prove it was his family," Laura said. "He doesn't talk."

"How old is he?" I asked.

"Seven, but he's tiny. Looks more like a four-year-old."

I stayed silent until my emotions settled down. Looking up I noticed the fixed glare on Laura's face. Was that why she came to Detroit—escaping home?

"What happened to your nose?" Ron asked.

"Got hit." I dropped my eyes.

"You fighting over money or a girl?" Phil quipped.

"Neither."

"Family matter?" Ron's eyebrows rose.

I turned back to Laura. "Where do you work?"

"Children's Hospital, downtown."

"You like it?"

"Sometimes. Not today."

I nodded. "That's how I felt in 'Nam. I loved savin' folks but hated watchin' people die."

Every head at the table swiveled toward me.

"You're a veteran?" Phil asked.

"Served three years."

"What'd you do?" Vic scrutinized my face.

"Navy corpsman. I went to school stateside for a year, worked a year on the hospital ship, and volunteered to work with the Marines."

"See any action?" Ron asked.

"Yeah."

They waited, but I didn't have any more to say. My reticence seemed to fuel their disapproval. They turned their heads away, ate in silence, and carried their dishes to the sink.

Vic took me aside after the meal. "Have you used drugs?"

I shook my head. "Unless you count a beer now and then."

"Do you object to other people using?"

I thought back to my mother, who'd been opiate addicted, and Jake, who'd been an alcoholic for years. I loved both people dearly, but their drugs nearly killed them. "They had opium in 'Nam, and some of my friends tried it, but from what I've seen, it's a very slippery slope. Once you're addicted, you're either gonna die or go to jail."

Vic studied me. "Are you a Narc?"

I almost laughed. No wonder I'd silenced the supper conversation. "No. I don't judge others unless their decisions affect me. But I hate losin' folks, especially good friends I've grown to love."

Vic's eyes widened, and he nodded. "Ditto that. Which leaves the decision in your hands."

Chapter 5

I brought my bag upstairs, luxuriating in a steamy shower and the opportunity to stretch out on a bed. The next day while nailing plywood to the rafters, I mulled over Vic's offer of a room. The plusses included a place I could afford with a friend from work and an interesting girl. The minuses included a couple homo druggies and a teenage hooker, any of whom might lead to trouble.

I knew what Red and Lee would say—no way, man. But what about Jake? He never judged other people, just let them be themselves, even when their behaviors could prove dangerous. Of course he'd been in prison, alcoholic, homeless, and had died because he failed to follow medical advice, but I still modeled my behavior after his. Unlike my father, Jake was always kind.

I'd measured an edge piece and went down to cut it, pushing the plywood through the blade, but the wood caught and jumped, the saw gouging my right hand. Pulling free, I grabbed my wrist, inspecting the damage—a deep, free-bleeding gash below my thumb. I thanked God I didn't lose it.

The Super brought a first-aid kit and studied the cut, then wrapped it tight to slow the blood. "Needs stitches," he said, supporting my assessment. "You got medical insurance?"

I shook my head, thinking I could sew it—if it wasn't on my hand. Vic climbed down and joined us. "I'll take you to the clinic," he offered. The Super waved us off.

I followed Vic to his car. "How much will they charge?"

"It's free, but they'll ask you to volunteer."

Vic didn't have to drive far. The clinic occupied the basement of a big office building on the west side of Woodward Avenue. The doctor only came on Tuesdays and Thursdays, and since this was a Thursday, I lucked out. I watched with interest as the nurse cleaned my wound and set up a sterile suture tray. A short Korean man entered the room, sat down, and introduced himself as Dr. Su.

He inspected my hand. "You one lucky guy; it miss tendon." He carefully sewed the muscle using gut and closed the skin with 5-0 nylon.

"Good job," I told him. "Thanks."

He looked surprised. "You medical student?

"No, Navy corpsman, but I learned to suture in the OR on the ship."

His eyes widened. "You corpsman? Want to volunteer? We need you here."

I shrugged, not sure that would be legal.

"Think about, please." He pulled out a script pad and wrote down his home number, handing it to me along with a script for Keflex. "Take one two time a day until you heal. How your nose?"

"It got broke a couple weeks back. The doctor told me to keep the splint on for six weeks."

"May I see?"

"Go ahead." The bruising had faded to purples and greens, and my face looked less swollen than it had. He peeled off the tape and lifted the splint so he could peer inside and feel the bone.

"Healing good but fragile. If hit now, do more than break—might kill you. Keep splint on and stay away from fight. I check in four week. Okay?" He frowned, his slanted eyes reminding me of Lee.

"Okay."

As Vic and I prepared to walk outside, Laura breezed in through the door.

"What happened?" she asked, eyes focused on my hand.

I grinned, unreasonably pleased by her concern. "Got klutzy with the saw, but it will heal. Dr. Su was great. He asked me to come help."

"Most of the roomies help out here." Laura glared at Vic. "Lou is the receptionist. Phil and Ron do repairs, and I work as a nurse. You could help with triage if you want." She kept her green eyes on Vic, and I saw more love than anger boiling deep inside. My grin faded.

"Tempting," I said. "So nobody cares if I don't have a license?"

She turned back to me, her eyes softening a tad. "No one pays attention, but it would look better if you were taking classes. Maybe toward your EMT?"

"I'll think on that." Meeting her gaze, I couldn't keep from smiling. What an idiot I was! She wanted Vic.

Back at the car, Vic popped the trunk and fished out a bottle. "Here's your Keflex."

"How much?"

"I'll settle for a buck; I get them free. By law, the pharmacies dispose of unsold pills once they reach their expiration date. They're usually effective for another year, and I sell them in a month for a whole lot less than any drugstore. But Laura wants me to supply the clinic free. I refused, and now she's pissed."

I nodded, puzzling on how much of that was truth. I suspected there might be a more personal betrayal behind the anger in those beautiful green eyes. "Will the Super keep me on?"

Vic smiled. "Yeah, he'll let you do cleanup, but you'll only get half-pay."

I sighed in relief. Back at the job site, I checked in. When the Super tossed a hardhat and pointed me toward a wheelbarrow and shovel, I was grateful for the work.

That night I ate and slept at the commune. The following day I got my pay, a measly forty-five dollars after taxes, but the sweetest cash I'd ever seen. I paid my rent, spent another ten on groceries, and five on toothpaste, soap, razorblades, and gauze squares to cover up the stitches in my hand. In my room, I stuffed all my clothes into the dresser, pinned my map to the wall, and felt at home.

When I tried to call Lee, I discovered our phone had no long-distance service. So I wrote a letter thanking him for giving me the gun—although I doubted I would use it—and asked him to give Ma my address. I couldn't bring myself to write her, knowing she read everything out loud to Pa. Picturing his face skewed with anger made me sick.

Chilling out at the house through the long summer evenings, I practiced sketching all my housemates. I drew Ron playing his guitar. He was a talented entertainer and his sweet tenor voice captivated everyone. One evening he chose songs from Simon and Garfunkel, and his performance of "The Boxer" moved me close to tears.

"You like music, Tennessee?" Ron smiled, his kindness relaxing my reserve.

"Ma's a singer, mostly gospel music, but I truly liked that song. It spoke to me."

"Any line in particular?"

I hesitated, but since I didn't see Ron as a threat, I replied, "The last line. The part where he says he's leaving but then stays."

Ron nodded, his brown eyes studying me closely. "Simon wrote that. What do you think it means?"

I met his gaze. "Life's tough, but even when you're wounded, you have to keep on fightin'."

Phil frowned at me, and I eyed him with concern, acutely aware of his relationship with Ron. Smiling, I asked, "Do you sing?"

He started laughing. "Like a tortured dog. You've got a good voice. Why don't you sing?"

I shrugged. I sang at my job, in the shower and car, and had harmonized with Ma in the privacy of home. But this was my home now, so I let Ron coax me into singing an old folk song, and the ensuing applause left me embarrassed but proud.

I sketched Phil distributing drugs to other housemates. Lou bought Dexedrine and phenobarbital. Anna took Quaaludes, and Vic pocketed the codeine.

"Because of an accident last year," he said to me.

Madge took a bag of pot, which she rolled up like a pro. Laura and I both abstained.

From memory I drew Vic working on the roof. They'd started nailing shingles, and Vic, a southpaw, showed me how to use the nail-gun left-handed. When the Super saw me nailing, he moved me to full pay, and I was stoked. As the weeks flew by, I fell into a rhythm of working with Vic, entertaining with Ron, and doing triage beside Laura at the clinic.

The clinic, like Vietnam, was either feast or famine. Some days no one came, and I sketched Laura—always cleaning up the place or helping other people. On days when we couldn't handle all the sick folk, I used everything I knew and learned everything I could. At those times, I longed to go to school.

One day an older woman brought a kid. He'd had a high fever and nausea for days. Outside of an IV, I didn't have a clue, but Laura immediately took blood and stool samples, obtained a history, and suggested foods he should avoid.

When they left, she told me to wash my hands now, and my clothes as soon as possible. "Did you notice the yellow in his eyes? I think he's got Hepatitis A, and that's contagious."

"Thanks." I followed her instructions, stripping down at home and doing my laundry in the basement washer. We didn't have a drier, so I hung my garments on the clothesline in the yard where the weeds and grass stood knee high. Checking inside the garage, I discovered a treasure trove of abandoned tools. I grabbed a hand mower and quickly did the lawn, used pruning shears on the bushes by the porch and a hammer and nails to fix the steps. Pleased with the results, I picked up all the mail and settled on the front porch, waiting for my roomies. In the pile, I found my license with a note:

Hi, Pete.

Hope your red Beetle made the trip okay. Glad to hear you found a job, a room, and made new friends. The gun was a gift for your 21st birthday. Sorry you won't be here to celebrate with me, but since you're in Detroit, you be watchful and stay safe. I'm out of school this summer, working as a legal clerk. If you need anything or want to talk, just call.

Your buddy, Lee

So typical of Lee—the worrier and fixer. But his words, even through a letter, soothed my soul. I leaned back against the railing, sun on my face, and I'd almost dozed off when I sensed movement near my car. Focusing my gaze, I noticed a small black kid carefully inspecting all the tires. I jumped off the porch and walked his way.

"You like my tires?'

The kid froze, staring up at me. "I don't mean no harm, man."

"Sure." I raised an eyebrow. "In case you don't know, I'm Pete. This is my car, and I live right over there." I nodded toward our house and crouched closer to his level. "I have a job for you."

He stood poised to run, but his dark eyes looked more curious than frightened.

"I need someone to watch out for my car. Interested?"

"How much it pay?"

"Not much, it's just for watchin' and tellin' me if there's any trouble. How much you think that's worth?"

"One dollar?"

"One dollar a week," I said. But I gotta know your name and where you live."

He grinned. "I'm Marcos, and I live the next block over, down that way." He pointed left.

"Okay, Marcos. Meet me by my car every Saturday at five. If it's still in one piece, you get paid." I held out my hand and he slapped it.

I watched him run across the street toward his home. He was quick and agile, reminding me a little of myself at that age. Finding a screwdriver, I attached the license, and returned to the veranda still chuckling to myself. It felt good to help a kid. Maybe he'd actually learn something, such as working for money is better than theft. Maybe not.

Laura arrived home as I was sketching Marcos. When I saw her arms loaded with heavy grocery bags, I put down my sketchpad and helped. We reached the kitchen and she sighed, as if exhausted beyond words.

"What's up?" I asked.

"Not much. I'm just worn out."

"Want me to put away the groceries?"

Her eyes widened in surprise. "You'd do that?"

"I used to help Ma all the time." I didn't tell Laura how much that had annoyed me, but she took me at my word and headed for the stairs. I'd about put the groceries away when Phil appeared.

"You fixing supper?"

I shrugged, searching through the groceries for something I could cook. "If you don't mind hamburgers with coleslaw."

"Works for me," Phil said. "Where are the girls?"

"Laura's upstairs—I think she crashed. Haven't seen Lou, and Marge isn't due home until six."

"What about Anna?"

I raised an eyebrow. "What's her story?"

"The usual: runaway, abusive home, sells her body to survive."

I dropped my eyes to the floor. If it hadn't been for Jake...

Phil stared at me a moment, studying my nose, and turned away.

I almost let him go but changed my mind. "Where you from?"

He faced me, glaring. "Detroit, hometown boy." His dark eyes narrowed, daring me to put him down.

"Parents?"

He scowled deeper.

I cocked my head, waiting.

He dropped his gaze and sighed. "Why you ask?"

"Well, Detroit's not Tennessee, but I expect folks here make all the same mistakes."

He checked my face and nodded. "That's a fact." Pivoting, he took the stairs two at a time.

I washed my hands again and shaped the ground beef into burgers, setting out buns, sliced onions and tomatoes. Searching through the freezer, I found some frozen French fries and lit the gas oven to heat up.

"You cooking?"

I spun before I recognized the voice. Lou had slipped silently behind me. Relaxing my fist, I laid the knife back on the counter and took a series of deep breaths.

Lou had backed up to the stairs, eyes wide. "You want me to leave or set the table?"

"The table. Thanks. Sorry. Where's Vic? I haven't seen him all day."

"Gone fishing." Her words sizzled like water in a hot frying pan.

I raised an eyebrow, pretty certain Vic's fish weren't edible. "Is that dangerous?"

Lou slapped the plates around without a word.

Everyone but Vic and Laura came down to eat, feasting in silence on my burgers, slaw, and fries. There were no compliments and no complaints, just a total lack of conversation. I suspected Vic's absence heralded a problem they could neither discuss nor put aside. I didn't ask.

Sunday arrived with Vic still missing. Dark bags formed half-moons underneath Lou's eyes. Ron and Phil kept whispering in corners, and Anna left her attic, repeatedly checking out the dining room for Vic. When Laura came downstairs, I cornered her.

"Do you know where Vic is?"

She sighed deeply while waiting for the toaster. "It's none of our business, Pete. Unless you're into drugs?" She glanced at me.

"Not me, but Vic sells. Is he in trouble?"

"He's always in trouble—takes far too many risks. Lou's pissed, but mostly 'cause she loves him."

"And you?"

She glared, but I could read the worry lines etched into her forehead. Vic attracted people like honey did flies. I had no intention of competing.

Laura's eyes gentled. "You don't know him well, do you?"

"Fill me in?"

Laura grabbed her toast and poured some juice. Sitting at the table, she finished the snack before she spoke. "Vic lost his parents early. He said his mom came from Jamaica, his dad from Canada, but someone murdered them both when he was young. He grew up on the street, doing what survivors do here—selling drugs. But Vic is smarter than most—finished high school on his own. After that he spent hours in the library, learning all he could about prescription medicine. Once he knew enough, he started selling. He did okay, bought this big old house, and started rescuing people off the street. He's brought home dozens through the years, including me."

With a small grin, I added myself to that long list. Laura grinned back and continued with her tale. "A year ago the cops arrested him. I don't know why, but they hurt him—bad. Since then, he's been using more narcotics, shooting up." She shook her head. "He can't afford it now, which leads to trouble."

"How'd they hurt him?"

"I don't know, but he had terrible pain and muscle spasms—couldn't sleep for weeks."

Shit! I knew living here could lead to trouble, but I chose it. Of course I didn't have much choice, not after someone took my money… Suddenly I added two plus two. "Vic stole my cash?"

Laura met my eyes. "That money saved his life, and he's tried very hard to pay you back. Vic's really a good guy, in his way."

I tensed my jaw and fists, feeling sick, but suddenly everything made sense. After my temper cooled, I had to admit my life was richer for his crime. "Where is he now?"

"In hiding."

I finished breakfast and retreated to my room. If Vic knew Detroit as well as I knew Walnut Springs, there was no way I could find him. But if he didn't show up by tomorrow, I might try.

Chapter 6

The next day I saw Vic on the job. I glared, and he avoided me. We'd progressed from roofing to wrapping up the building, which kept my hands busy while my mind processed his theft. Laura said the money saved his life, and he tried hard to pay me back. That sounded good, but would I steal from him, even if my life was on the line?

Of course Vic lost both his parents early and had a hard struggle just to stay alive. Considering all that, he was surprisingly kind, and he'd helped me every chance he had. An aura about him drew other people in—aside from his good looks, intelligence, and kindness. Born in a different place, he might have been a leader instead of an addict selling drugs.

By lunchtime, Vic had disappeared. In the parking lot, I glimpsed him near his car and wandered over. Hearing his voice, I stopped and crouched behind a truck.

"Hurting me won't get you any money. I've always paid you—usually on time. Give me another week, and I'll have it all."

I straightened up enough to case the enforcer, a large piece of muscle grasping a metal pipe, and I flipped instantly to battle mode. Hyper-alert, I checked around for weapons—nothing near. Then I recalled Lee's gun. Moving close to the ground, I slunk back to my car and retrieved the .45 from the trunk. While sneaking back, I loaded in the bullets.

Vic screamed, and I ran toward them. He was on the ground when the enforcer struck again. I heard bones crack as Vic yelped.

"Stop or I'll shoot." I stood, leveling my gun at the attacker. He ignored me and raised the pipe to land another blow. Time slowed as I fell into familiar routines: steady, aim carefully, draw and hold your breath. I saw Vic's right hand reaching in slow motion for the pistol that had dropped from his left. As his fingers grasped the handle, I squeezed my trigger. Our two shots rang out almost as one.

The enforcer fell, clutching at his chest. Voices and running feet echoed from the work site. "Call an ambulance!" I yelled. "Two men down!"

Holstering my gun inside my boot, I played out the familiar role of medic. Vic lay groaning, his left hand a mangled mess, his right thigh bent at an awkward angle with a bone fragment sticking through his pants. Neither wound bled excessively, and with no morphine or splints, there was little I could do.

"The ambulance is comin'," I told Vic. "Just lie still."

"Take the gun," he whispered. Reaching up with his pistol, he froze, cursing. I quickly grabbed the gun, set the safety, and stuck it down in my other boot.

As construction workers reached the site, I turned away from Vic to check our target. His blood was spurting out and pooling on the ground. One bullet had entered his left chest, and the other found his right shoulder—where I'd aimed. He appeared to have a heart wound—unlikely he'd reach the hospital alive. For appearances only, I rolled up my t-shirt and applied pressure to his chest.

An ambulance arrived, and the paramedics took control. They filled Vic full of morphine, splinted his leg and hand, and placed him inside the ambulance. A second team attempted to stem the flow of blood still pulsing from the enforcer's chest. I already knew he was dead.

As the ambulance drove off, I snapped out of battle mode. Hearing more sirens in the distance, I panicked. Police! What had I done? Did I kill him? Had military training kicked in at the end and placed my bullet in his chest? I'd killed men during war, but this was *murder*.

I fled to my car and headed for the commune, picked up all my gear, and quickly drove into the country. *Coward!* hissed inside my head, but I pushed that aside and struggled back to logic. Had anybody seen me with the gun? Should I turn myself in? What did I know about the dead man? For certain he had bosses, drug lords who would try to track us down. I didn't know how powerful those drug lords might be, or how much pressure they could bring to bear. My best bet was probably to run. Or was it? I could say I heard shots and found both men on the ground. Running was the surest sign of guilt—and cowardice.

I followed the road signs to a nearby lake, its beach deserted on a Monday. Picking up my fishing pole, I walked out to the point. After checking carefully in all possible directions,

I hurled the guns as far as I could throw. The ripples widened, crossing one another, until they formed wavelets at the shore. I meandered down the shoreline, casting my line from time to time, and ended my walk back at the car.

Calmer now, I drove into Detroit, stopping at the hospital nearest to our work—Detroit General. Known locally as DGH, it housed the trauma center for the city. The front-desk clerk located Vic in the OR. I found the cafeteria and bought myself a hotdog. Seated by the wall, I ate while carefully watching all the people. Policemen and security guards wandered in and out, but no obvious enforcers. When I returned to the desk, the clerk said Vic was already in Recovery. I followed the signs upstairs and stopped outside the locked double doors. A waiting room stood empty right across the hall. Unable to sit, I started pacing.

I knew Vic had bad fractures in his hand and leg, and it would take months for him to heal—assuming he could stay alive that long. Would the enforcers come for him in the hospital or would they wait 'til he got home? I didn't want any part of a drug war, but how could I abandon my new friends?

I paced until a nurse unlocked the double doors. She asked for friends and relatives of Victor Dumont, and I followed her back to a small room. Dressed in the standard OR gown, Vic lay on a cot, IV in his arm, O_2 in his nose. The surgeon had placed his broken leg in traction and wrapped his left hand in a cast.

"Vic?" I laid my hand on his right arm.

He opened his eyes, staring. "Tennessee?" he whispered. "What you doing?"

"Checkin' on you."

Vic kept staring, hazel eyes dilated, eyebrows raised as if asking me a question.

"I didn't do it. You did," I explained. "Straight through the heart."

His face cleared, and he nodded.

"How you feel?"

"Like shit." He closed his eyes again, losing his battle to the anesthesia. I waited quietly 'til he resurfaced. Vic whispered, "Will I heal?"

I could have lied, but now his eyes held steady, demanding the full truth. "That depends on your surgeon."

He turned his head away with a soft sigh. When the surgeon arrived, I felt relieved to see a smile.

"Dr. Ridgewood," he said, extending his hands to Vic and me.

"I'm Pete Martin, Vic's friend." I shook hands, impressed by his firm grip.

Turning to Vic, Dr. Ridgewood explained, "I put a pin in your femur to stabilize the fracture, and you'll be in traction for at least a couple weeks. After that I hope we can put you in a cast and send you home. If everything goes smoothly, your leg should heal. Your hand took more damage. It has multiple fractures and crushed tissue—lots of little bones with tendons, nerves, and vessels. I did the best I could, but you can't use it for at least six more weeks, and some parts may need more surgery."

Vic bit his lower lip. "That's my working hand."

"I know." The surgeon met Vic's worried gaze. "I spliced a nerve together in an effort to save it, but nerves can take several months to heal."

As soon as the surgeon left the room, Vic turned to me. Motioning me closer, he hissed, "If that shit-head had given me more time, I could've paid."

"I'm really sorry, Vic, but you know it's not my fight."

"It is now," he snorted. "If anybody saw, you're in deep shit."

Is he blackmailing me? I doubted Vic would do that, but I couldn't be sure, not with his life on the line.

"Just listen," Vic said. "I have a buyer for a kilo of pure heroin. That alone would more than pay my debts."

"Where would you get it?"

"That's the gig. It's sitting in a warehouse right across the bridge." He raised an eyebrow, and I knew what he was asking.

"You want me to save you after you stole all my money?" I scowled deeply.

Vic sighed and dropped his gaze, but after a minute, he met my angry stare. "If I don't pay them now, they're gonna kill me and quite possibly go after you as well." He nodded to the traction rig, his hand. "You can run, but I'm stuck. They can kill me anytime."

"You're crazy." But even as I said that, I remembered the enforcer aiming his next blow at Vic's head. "Why would they kill you?"

The lines deepened in his face. "I know too much." He paused, drawing a deep, ragged breath. "That gang is famous for its violence, always has been. One of their enforcers killed my folks, and I've been tracking him for years. Had him in my sights, but it seems they got me first. The cops…" His leg cramped and he gasped, a grimace freezing his face.

I took his hand, and he grabbed hard, panting. I pulled free to find a nurse, and she followed me back, carrying a loaded hypodermic. After checking his nametag and filling out her forms, she emptied it into his IV.

As Vic relaxed, I sat beside him, trying to reason a way out. But he'd convinced me his death was imminent, and I'd lost too many friends to turn away. I felt trapped.

After the nurse left, I checked on Vic again, and his eyes opened at my touch. In spite of the morphine, he still looked to be in pain. I took his uninjured hand in mine. "How do you feel?"

"I'm okay," he said, but his lips pursed tight.

"How much money do you need?"

"More than you've got." He held his voice barely above a whisper. "The only way to raise it is to sell the heroin. I've tried three times to pick it up, but I was tailed."

"Why not Phil?"

Vic pulled back. "He's got a rap sheet that stretches from here to Florida. If he's caught, they'll send him up for life."

"What are the odds of gettin' caught?"

"At the bridge? One in thirty."

I sighed, my stomach tied in knots. "I'm a greenhorn, Vic. You certain you want me?"

Vic studied my face. "You'll do fine. Once I pay my debt, we'll split the profits fifty-fifty."

I shrugged. The money didn't register with me. "When do you need it?"

A haze descended over Vic, and his words began to slur. "I think they'll lie low…wait a week…July first?"

The nurse reappeared to check his vitals, and shortly two orderlies walked in. I stood back, let them do their jobs, and followed the parade down the hallway. Since Vic couldn't pay, his bed was placed in a ward, which already housed five men.

I cased his roommates, but as far as I could tell, they were all equally impaired. When the staff left again, I whispered in his ear, "At least you have witnesses. I'll check out the other, let you know."

Vic barely squeezed my hand, his eyes now closed.

Chapter 7

Phil, Ron, and I split shifts for guarding Vic. Mine started after work and went 'til midnight. Next day at the construction site, I listened in on gossip. Everyone was talking about Vic and the enforcer, but no one acted suspiciously toward me. I told the Super that Vic was in traction and wouldn't work for several months. Many of the workers had bought medicine from Vic, and they stopped to offer money and support. If any of them were aware of my involvement, they kept that information to themselves.

Gaining confidence, I returned to nailing plywood to the floor joists. I left work an hour early and crossed the bridge to Windsor, observing the border crossing protocols up close. It was, as Vic promised, randomly patrolled. From time to time, they pulled a car aside, but when they searched, they did a thorough job.

There were other options, like boats. The Coast Guard policed the river crossings, but with so many miles of rivers and lakes, their cruisers couldn't watch them all. I knew nothing about boats and would need to hire both a boat and a crew. That required money and increased our risk. I chose the bridge.

Vic said the merchandise was stored in a locker inside a warehouse near the lake. I'd need to hide it in my car, and there wasn't much room inside a Beetle. The spare tire was far too obvious, as were areas behind fenders, bumpers, and underneath the frame. Would it fit into the dash—either behind or beside the radio? That would take time and tools to install, but it would be more difficult to find.

When I returned to DGH, Vic looked tense.

"Hey, Vic, how you doin'?"

"The cops came."

His right hand was trembling, and I touched his arm. "What did you tell them?"

He bit down on his lip. "I said I couldn't remember a damn thing."

Eyeing the pained grimace on his face, I chose not to push him. "Lighten up. It's my birthday."

Vic relaxed and met my gaze. "Which one?"

"My twenty-first."

"No shit!" Vic almost smiled. "Damn! Wish I could offer you a drink."

"You gave me a present. Once it arrives, what should I do?"

Vic's eyes lit up. "You gonna go?"

I nodded. "Then what?"

"Tell Phil. I'll give him the details, and he'll arrange the rest." Vic grinned like a little kid.

I picked the coming Friday, June 30, for the trip, hoping holiday traffic would reduce my chances for a search. In Windsor, I found the brick exactly where Vic said. Removing the radio,

I fit the heroin behind it, but the wires couldn't reach around. I hunted under both hoods until I found the heater, removed those wires, and spliced them in. Reconnected, the radio turned on, but it crackled. I hadn't thought to bring electrical tape.

At precisely five p.m. I drove onto the highway into preholiday rush-hour traffic. The bridge lanes moved slower than expected, and it took me a half-hour just to reach the gate. As I crawled forward, I downed a beer and kept a close watch on the search area ahead. They hadn't pulled anybody over for a while, and my odds grew shorter with each car.

I'd bought a stash of snacks and water for the trip and kept munching down as I approached. I was eating far too much, but it helped calm me. When I finally reached the window and handed over my license, the lady kept it. "Please move your car over to the side, sir. Right there." She pointed to the dreaded spot.

I moved my car, and two heavily muscled men came to the door. "Please get out, sir. Leave the keys."

I walked to the railing, staring upriver to the skyline of Detroit. Behind me I heard the radio turn on, crackling with static, and my heart jumped to my throat. I kept staring at the city, praying to arrive there without handcuffs.

After several minutes, I dared to turn around and watch the men as they checked out the tires, exhaust, and undercarriage. To double check, they brought a dog to sniff the car. The heroin was triple bagged, but would that be enough? Nausea overcame me and I heaved, hanging over the railing to unload my full stomach into the river far below. One of the searchers touched my shoulder. I flinched, fists clenched around the rail.

"Are you sick, sir?"

I nodded. "Hope it's not hepatitis. I work in the ER, and we've seen a lot of hepatitis A."

He removed his hand quickly and stepped back. "We're almost done." Then he called off the dogs and brought my keys. "Are you okay to drive, sir?"

"Yeah." I wiped the vomit on my sleeve, and he backed up farther, motioning me into my car.

I rejoined the traffic, sweating as though I'd been humping across 'Nam. When I reached the Detroit side, I drove straight home and parked, leaving the heroin where even the searchers couldn't find it. Upstairs I stripped down and took a cool shower until my pulse and breathing normalized.

Someone knocked while I was drying off. "Just a sec!" I yelled.

"You've got a visitor," Laura answered from the hall.

"Who?"

"Some little kid."

I wrapped a towel around me and stepped into the hall. Laura moved back, staring at my muscled body. Turning fast to hide more than my smile, I entered my room and closed the door.

Dressed, I hurried downstairs and found Marcos in the parlor. "Hey Dude, almost payday?" We bumped fists, slapped hands, and I slipped him a buck. "How's my car?"

"Some guy's been watchin' it ever since ya got here."

"Really?" I sat on the floor, patting the cushion next to me. "What's he look like?"

"Big white guy, kinda tough."

"Is he packin'?"

Marcos nodded.

"Does he live around here?"

"No, he drives a Charger, all black."

"Is he out there now?"

Marcos glided to the windows and glanced up and down the street. "Nope."

"Good job." I gave him another dollar bill and sent him home.

Someone must have picked up on my smuggling. It was past time to give the merchandise to Phil. I ran upstairs and knocked loudly on his door. No one was home, so I walked in. Turning my back on the messy, king-sized bed, I stood behind the drapes and watched the street. After almost five minutes, a black Charger cruised by, slowed, and turned around the block. I checked my watch, and after seven more minutes, he returned. The next round took eight, but by then I knew it was an interval patrol, and I knew exactly what to do.

I went out to the garage and studied the old tools. Closing the door, I quickly organized the floor space until I saw the Charger make another round. Once he left, I drove my car inside and closed the door. Back inside the house, I waited by the parlor window, and on the next round the Charger slowed. From that man's perspective, I'd just driven out of sight. I watched in amusement as he sped toward Woodward in a vain attempt to catch me.

Back in the garage, I removed the drugs and rewired my car, ears on alert. I brought a pry-bar and hammer to my room, loosened a floorboard, and hid the brick underneath. Pacing nervously, I waited there.

As I paced, I recalled an earlier conversation when I'd briefed Phil about my plans. He knew I would leave at 5 p.m., but the trip had taken much longer than expected. Had he gone in search of me, or had he sold me out? Vic trusted Phil completely, but I didn't. He might have set up his own meeting with the buyer.

Knowing those concerns were out of my control, I picked up my sketchpad and started drawing Laura, capturing her expression while staring at my pecs. But even that distraction didn't calm me. I didn't know Phil's history, except what Vic had said about his rap sheet. Was he a drug dealer or a thief? Did he truly value Vic, or did he harbor dreams of being boss?

It was dark before Phil returned. I heard his boots on the stairs and a knock on my door. Looking through the keyhole, I recognized his face and opened up.

"You got it?"

"Yep." I removed the floorboard and handed him the brick, praying Vic's judgment was sound. "You need back-up?"

Phil looked over in surprise, as if he'd forgotten I had military training. "Naw, I got Ron and we'll be fine. But thanks."

Phil trotted downstairs, and the front door slammed shut. I watched from the window as he joined Ron in their truck. Taking a deep breath, I relaxed, relieved my part in this drug deal was now over. I glanced across the hall, saw Laura in her room, and moved toward her. "I'm off to see Vic. Any messages?"

She looked up with a smile that almost made me stay. "Thanks for helping. I know you don't approve, but Vic deserved a break." She stood up and planted a kiss on my right cheek. "Be careful."

For a minute, being careful was the last thing on my mind. I barely managed to leave, staggering downstairs in a daze. Did she offer that kiss for me, or Vic? Still befuddled, I walked out to the garage.

A man jumped me from behind, hands around my neck. Dropping under him, I lifted up, but it took all my strength to throw him off me. He hit the ground hard, and I kicked him in the head. Peering through the darkness, I saw a husky white man, maybe thirty, about 250 pounds, and guessed he was the same guy Marcos saw. For the time being, he lay motionless but breathing. Running to my car, I drove straight to DGH, expecting the enforcer would soon follow.

Inside the hospital, surrounded by security, I stood watching and waiting for my tail. After ten or fifteen minutes, I relaxed, walked upstairs, and checked out the nursing station before heading to Vic's room. But as I glanced inside the ward, my heart sank. An older white man leaned against the far wall, a pistol partially concealed between his hands. Shit!

Seeing me, the old guy took a seat, as if he were a relative or friend. But his eyes kept checking out the patients and the hall.

I darted over to the desk clerk and whispered, "There's an old white guy in the ward with a gun."

She called security while I kept a cautious watch. Within minutes, a team of cops stormed through. I followed to the doorway as they surrounded him. The old guy handed them his pistol and accepted his arrest quietly. Once they were gone, I hurried to Vic's side.

His face relaxed once he saw me. "You're late."

"Who was the white guy with the gun?"

Vic stared at me, eyes wide. "Is that why the cops came?"

I realized Vic couldn't turn around, his movement limited by the traction rig. That had to terrify him. I pulled up a chair and told him in a whisper how the two men searched my car, how the Dodge Charger kept watch around the block, and about the hefty white guy who jumped me.

"Did Phil get the merchandise?"

"Yeah."

I waited with Vic until Phil arrived near midnight. Like any good sergeant, he reported in. "It's done."

Vic snorted. "Not the payoff. Until that happens, we're all very much at risk."

I glanced at Phil. "You know an old white guy with a moustache, thinning hair? He was behind Vic with a gun."

Phil shook his head as worry creased his forehead. His eyes stayed steady on Vic's face, reading him before he glanced appraisingly at me. "I'll stay for the night shift. You guard the house. The cash is where you hid the brick, and Ron has extra guns."

I raised an eyebrow at that sign of trust and headed home.

Chapter 8

Before Phil had a chance to make the payoff, the hospital chose to discharge Vic. They took him out of traction and put him in a cast that went all the way to his waist on the right. That meant he couldn't sit up, stand, walk, or take care of his most basic needs. All those jobs were dumped into our hands.

Anna took the call. By the time I got off work, the house was total chaos. Lou transformed the parlor into a bedroom suite, using the sofa as a bed, and she completed her decor with a bedside commode. Ron and Phil were busy hanging drapes across the archway to give Vic a façade of privacy, and Anna was on the phone searching for a walker to help Vic move around the house.

"At least he'll have a nurse." Phil winked at Laura.

I raised an eyebrow, meeting Laura's stare. We both knew that Vic would be bedbound for at least a month and need round the clock nursing care.

Vic arrived late that evening, two paramedics carrying his stretcher up the steps and into the front room. They dumped him there, half-on, half-off the sofa, and left. Phil and I turned him so the cast was near the sofa back, his left leg along the front where he could bend it to the floor.

After the girls had greeted him and left, I closed the curtains and brought Vic an empty bottle. He peed and handed it to me. "Thanks! I hate being such a pest."

"No problem. Glad you're home." I emptied the bottle and returned, pulling a chair up next to him. "Havin' all that money in the house makes me nervous. What's your plan?"

"They're coming here."

"Here? When?" I couldn't believe he'd invited those thugs into our house.

"Tomorrow evening. In the meantime, I suggest you take half our funds and put them in a bank—in your name."

That made more sense. "Okay, I can do that. How much should I leave?"

Vic gave that question serious thought. "I owed them ten thou plus interest, which means it doubles every week. It's almost two weeks since they attacked, so that would make it forty grand. But I think they'll settle for twenty-five plus change."

"What if they don't? You got a gun?"

He shrugged. "I have guns, but I don't plan to use them. I have something they want far more than money."

"Information?" I guessed.

"You're too smart, Tennessee. I know you got my back, but stay out of the negotiations. Promise?"

I nodded. "How far out? Out of the room, out of the house?"

"Stay upstairs in your own room, door closed. This is privileged information and knowing it would put your life at risk—like mine."

I sat and thought, suspecting he might offer a supplier, maybe where he got the heroin. "Are you goin' out of business?"

Vic sighed and shook his head. "I'm paying off a debt, okay. Please stop asking questions." He narrowed his eyes, but they weren't angry—more imploring.

"Okay. How much money in the bank?"

"Twenty-five."

Early the next morning, I took five packets of five thousand dollars each and drove directly to the nearest bank. Explaining that my uncle had just died, I requested an account and deposited the money. The cashier didn't even raise an eyebrow. There must be oodles of dead uncles in Detroit, and I wondered what percent made their money selling cars and what percent selling drugs.

I returned to the house and handed Vic the bankbook. He studied the figures and gave it back to me. Pocketing the book, I drove to work, arriving late. The Super looked pissed until I told him Vic was home. His eyes softened as he asked about Vic's health, shaking his head in sympathy. But in the blink of an eye his face hardened, and he said if I missed one minute more, he'd dock my pay.

The weather heated up, and I went through water as if my skin had sprung a leak. That reminded me of 'Nam, but I told myself repeatedly it wasn't that hot, and I had plenty to drink. I still stayed antsy, and part of that was due to the evening's preparations. As we finished up the flooring, I wished I had somewhere else to go.

Back home I ate and showered, aware of the silent tension in the house. Phil and Ron had barricaded their room above the parlor, and I guessed they had peepholes in the floor. I'd just run downstairs to check on Vic when a long black limo pulled up outside our house. Vic tensed and pointed toward my room. I retreated in a hurry, slamming and locking my bedroom door behind me. Stretching out on the hardwood, I pressed my ear against the crack.

I heard the front door open and multiple footsteps on the wooden floor. My best guess at a headcount was four men. From his bed on the sofa, Vic greeted his guests and invited them to join him in the parlor. Chairs squeaked and scraped as men dragged them across the floor.

"Thank you for coming. I'd have met you at your place, but as you well know, I'm indisposed," Vic began.

I winced at the obvious sarcasm.

"We came to collect, not socialize," a bass voice responded, its tone rough and rude.

"I'd like to offer a different type of payment."

"What type?"

"A letter of introduction." I heard the crinkle of paper as the offer exchanged hands, followed by silence.

The bass voice finally spoke. "You owed us ten thou two weeks back, but since you've been 'indisposed', I'm willing to reduce your interest rate and accept thirty thou with the address for this letter."

"I can give you twenty thou plus the address, but only if you guarantee my safety and the safety of the people in my household," Vic replied.

"If we reach an agreement, that guarantee is made, but not for less than thirty thou."

Vic stayed quiet. By this time, I'd figured out what Ron and Phil had planned and feared the scene would quickly escalate. I had no doubt that the other side brought backup, and I only had Ron's .38.

A different voice spoke from the parlor, a tenor with a slight Italian twang. "It might benefit both sides to accept a compromise of twenty-five thou plus the address."

I breathed out.

"That's our final offer," the bass voice said.

"I accept your offer with your guarantee of safety," Vic replied.

I heard footsteps coming down the hall and a gentle knock on my door. "It's me, Phil."

I peered through the keyhole and opened up the door.

"I need the money," Phil whispered, as I closed the door behind him.

I nodded. "Should I follow?"

"No. Vic wants you out of sight." He handed me the M-14.

I held onto that treasure as Phil opened up the floorboards and fished out the cash. He counted it twice and headed down the stairs. The transactions below diminished into silence, except for faint sounds of shuffling bills and soft whispers. Scraping chairs and footsteps followed shortly.

"I'll hold you to your promises," Vic said.

"And I'll hold you to yours." The Italian's inflection hinted at a threat, but before I could react, the front door slammed.

I let out a shaky breath. From my room, I couldn't see the limo, but Ron walked past and gave the all-clear sign. I followed downstairs, rifle in hand.

"Well done, Vic," Phil said. "You got those devils off our back, and now we can manage our own horse."

"Thanks to Tennessee." Vic glanced in my direction. "I need to talk with him. Alone." He raised an eyebrow at Phil and Ron. Phil grabbed the M-14, and he and Ron went outside on the porch.

I sat by Vic. "You startin' somethin' new?"

"You want in?"

I shook my head. "I won't smuggle. That's a one-way ticket into prison."

Vic chuckled. "You don't need to smuggle. I want you to guard my back. You've been doing that for free and deserve to get paid." He grabbed my arm, eyes meeting mine. "If you don't want in, I understand. But you did your part well, so keep the cash either way."

I stared at him. "All of it? It's mine?"

Vic laughed. "You're a hoot, Tennessee. If you joined us, you'd make millions."

"What are you sellin'?"

"Same as before, but I've added heroin. I need it and can't afford to get in debt again."

I thought about Ma and shook my head.

Vic nodded. "Okay. But the other side already thinks you're in, so you're not immune to all the risks."

Chapter 9

A t first nothing changed. I went to my construction job at 8 a.m. each morning, came home, showered, and shared supper at the house. I didn't worry as much about my paycheck, spending it more freely than I had before. Among my purchases, I bought another handgun—an M1911 semi-automatic pistol—same as I'd carried back in 'Nam.

The heat wave continued to oppress us. It enveloped the city like a fog, inciting rage and dulling the cognition of everyone who trudged up and down the streets. At work I heard more arguments, more violence in the threats. At the clinic, our clients grew impatient, cussing us out about long waits. At home a tense silence filled the air.

The last Sunday in July, I slept late and finished up some sketches before heading down for brunch. I met Laura on the stairs, her green eyes wide and staring.

"What's wrong?" I asked.

"They're rioting on Twelfth Street, burning and looting." She pointed to my window where I clearly saw the smoke.

"That's walkin' distance," I said, wondering if the violence might spread.

"The clinic will be busy—can you come?" Her voice trembled.

"Let's eat first."

Back in my room, I pocketed my gun. Downstairs, Laura was already in the kitchen making sandwiches for us both. I grabbed a beer as she turned on the news.

"The riot in Detroit has been contained in the city, cordoned off by the police. Firefighters attempting to put out the fires have been met with bottles, rocks, and even bullets, forcing them to retreat behind the lines. As we speak, the rioters are breaking store windows, stealing whatever they can carry and setting fire to the rest. Without police and firefighters there, the flames are spreading and the violence escalating. If you are in that area, you are highly advised to stay inside."

"That area includes us." My anger surged as I realized the police and firefighters had abandoned us to the mob violence and flames. "When did it start?"

Laura looked up from her food. "Late last night. The cops arrested a large group of people partying in a blind pig down off Twelfth Street. The street folks clearly disapproved. I don't know who sparked the violence, but now that it's lit, no one can stop it."

"Blind pig?" I raised a questioning eyebrow.

Laura wrinkled up her nose. "An unlicensed bar, like a speakeasy but with gambling, drugs, and girls."

The air outside felt sultry, promising worse heat by afternoon. Our street appeared deserted as we hiked east toward Woodward. At the corner store, a band of street kids rummaged through clothes they'd stolen off the racks. I ignored them. Farther down Woodward, shattered glass littered the sidewalk, and a larger group of young black toughs was looting amps and speakers from a window display.

One tall kid, acting as their leader, stepped in front of me with a defiant stare. "Where ya going, Whitey?" He flaunted a switchblade. "Your lady friend looks sweet—like cotton candy." He licked his lips and made a kissing noise. Encouraged by his boldness, the other kids moved close, blocking our way.

I pushed Laura behind me, but she turned toward the kids. "We work at the clinic. If you'll let us through, we'll be there when you need us."

The tall kid eyed his troops. "We don't need no babysitters, Sugar." Sneering at Laura, he thrust his knife toward my face.

I grabbed his wrist with my left hand, twisting 'til the knife clattered onto the street. With my right hand, I found my gun. Raising it so everyone could see, I forced my would-be attacker to his knees. The crowd parted like the red sea, and I led Laura through.

At the clinic, Dr. Su let us inside. The waiting room was filled, and he was trying his best to maintain some kind of order. I found myself ten thousand miles away, labeling the wounded for evacuation. The piled bodies were Priority V. I gave morphine to the dying guy who lost both his legs. He wouldn't make it—

Priority IV. The walking wounded crowded around me. I kept an eye on them—Priority III—as I continued to stabilize the Priority I and II casualties waiting for the chopper.

As Laura rushed in to assist Dr. Su, my mind snapped back into the present. Climbing on a table, I announced, "If you're bleedin' bad, come forward. If you can't breathe or you're havin' chest pain, please come forward."

A tiny black lady made her way to the front, and a man limped up, dripping blood.

I stared down at the little lady. "What's wrong?"

"My son's dyin'." She nodded toward a bench near the back.

I caught Laura's eye and nodded at the bleeding man. Jumping down, I followed the lady through the crowd. The young man stretched out on a bench appeared unconscious, barely breathing, his clothes soaked with blood.

"What happened?" I peeled back his shirt.

"He got knifed."

I raised an eyebrow, wondering if I'd disarmed his attacker. Maybe I should have kept the knife.

The wound oozed blood. "Can somebody please bring soap and water, and grab a pressure cuff and stethoscope as well." An older man stood and headed toward the back.

As I washed the wound, I feared the knife had nicked his heart, although he wasn't bleeding heavily. "How long ago?" I asked.

"'Most an hour."

If it was a heart wound, he'd be dead. Once the cuff arrived, I discovered his pressure was near normal. I listened with the stethoscope and heard a hissing sound. Checking out his wound, I saw air bubbling and realized he had a punctured lung.

"I need oxygen, a mask, and some clean plastic wrap with waterproof tape." This time his mother made the trip.

The oxygen brought her son around. He watched while I rigged an airtight dressing. "Take it easy," I told him, as he struggled to sit up, "or you might collapse that lung." When I finished, I turned toward the crowd. "Anybody willin' to drive him to the ER?"

The man who'd limped to the front raised his hand. He was sitting on a table while Dr. Su sutured his wound. When the doctor finished, Laura wrapped the injured foot. Several helpers carried the knife victim to the truck, and I helped the driver to his cab.

"Thanks for takin' him," I said. "Drive carefully."

"Thank *you*." He waved and headed off toward DGH.

Laura joined me at the door. "I hope they get there in one piece."

I recalled the barricades and sighed.

By mid-afternoon, I felt totally exhausted, partially from the heat, but mostly in my mind. The wounds I saw were cuts— not bullet wounds, the victims black residents—not soldiers. But I still kept seeing images from 'Nam.

As I chugged a glass of water, I watched another local family hurrying inside. They joined a growing group of refugees.

"We'll need to feed them," I told Laura.

Dr. Su joined us, his intelligent mind considering the options. "I know Chinese restaurant." He went to the phone and spoke at length with the owner. "The restaurant closed, but he have food. He agree to give us, but need a volunteer to bring it."

For some unknown reason, they all turned to me—even Laura. I suddenly wished I'd brought my car. "The restaurant three block down Woodward, that way." Dr. Su pointed to the south. "Called Royal Ming."

I left, walking quickly until rifle fire rattled not a block away. I sprinted, praying my white skin didn't mark me as a target. I reached the restaurant, out of breath but unscathed, and an older Chinese man opened the door.

"You Pete?"

"Yeah." I stepped inside, and he locked the door behind me. As I caught my breath, the aroma of Chinese food overwhelmed my nose and my stomach started growling noisily. "Sorry."

The owner smiled and dished up a warm bowl of rice mixed with eggs and other goodies. I dug in as though I'd just finished a forced march, and, as always, eating calmed me. After I'd devoured every morsel, he covered a table with large paper boxes, filling them with cooked meats, vegetables, and rice. "You need service?"

I guessed at what he meant. "I need plates, or bowls, maybe fifty of them, and somethin' to eat with." I gestured with my hands.

He nodded, bringing me a stack of paper plates followed by a bag of forks.

"Cups too." I mimed drinking.

He added those, and we carried the food and supplies out to his truck, parked in back. He handed me the keys. "Be careful. Stay in alley."

"You're not comin'? How will you get your truck?"

"Dr. Su say you bring it back."

I hadn't counted on that but didn't argue. Driving slowly, I saw a group of scruffy black men carrying boxes of merchandise out into the alley. Another group loaded the goods into a truck. Some of the men glared threateningly at me. I kept moving. Reaching the clinic, I parked, stepped out, and banged hard on the back door. When Laura opened up, her eyes flashed a welcome that almost made up for the trip. I handed her the food and carried in supplies while she arranged them cafeteria style. As she and Dr. Su stood dishing out the portions, Laura glanced questioningly at me.

"I have to take the truck back."

Smiling at her frown, I took off. Driving slowly down the alley, I watched an elegant white Lincoln pull up beside an unmarked door. A portly, gray-haired black man clambered out, carrying a large ring of keys. He probably owned the shop, so I drove on.

Two gunshots rang out loudly. Glancing in my mirror, I saw the owner stagger and fall. I stopped the truck and jumped out, but two masked men with guns appeared from out of nowhere. Heart pounding, hands sweating, I sprang back in the cab and hit the gas. At the next street, I turned right, taking a circuitous route back to the restaurant.

Parking the truck, I breathed out in relief. The old Chinese man opened up his back door, took his truck keys, and bowed. "Thank you very much."

"Thank you for the food." I bowed back. Leaving by the front door, I raced all the way down Woodward. I was breathing hard by the time I reached the clinic. Laura's smile returned when she looked up.

"Saw a man shot…two men came with guns…couldn't do a thing," I explained between gasps.

"Call 911?" Dr. Su suggested.

Laura dialed, but the line beeped busy. After a couple dozen tries, she called the cops, who promised they would send somebody out.

"What about tonight?" I asked, eyeing all the people gathered in the front.

"We're also low on medical supplies." Laura handed me a list, and I added food, toilet paper, and diapers to the page. Retreating to the back storage room, I relaxed and puzzled over how to get supplies. We needed an outsider, someone with the resources to buy and bring provisions for at least a couple days. Moving to the desk, I called our house.

"Hi Anna. Is Vic with you?" I waited while she brought him the phone.

"Hey, Tennessee." Vic's voice sounded cheerful. "Where are you?"

"Laura and I are at the clinic, and we have a crowd of maybe fifty refugees. We need food, but also diapers, toilet paper, blankets, antibiotics, suture kits, and bandages of all kinds. You know anyone who can buy all that and bring it?"

I waited until Vic said, "Let me make some calls. I'll call you back."

It was barely five minutes when the phone rang again. I answered, relieved to hear Vic's voice.

"A group of men with rifles and a truck should be at your back door in a couple hours. Might work better if you had some black folks meet them. These guys are black nationalist militants."

"How militant?"

Vic chuckled. "They won't shoot you, but they might call you names. Just stay cool."

I shared the plan with Dr. Su and Laura, and they asked for volunteers to unload supplies. I saw a few raised hands and told them to be ready in about two hours. That accomplished, I asked if anybody else needed medical attention, and a few more people raised their hands. I motioned them up front and began triage.

As sunset approached, the heat increased from hot to stifling, and the sporadic pop of rifles warned us of the dangers still outside. The refugees settled into family groupings, encouraging their little ones to sleep. Dr. Su went home, promising to return early Tuesday, which left Laura and me on our own.

"You want to go back home?" I asked. "It might be safer there."

She shrugged. "You?"

"I'd better stay. If no one's here, they'll loot all our supplies."

"You can't stop a mob, Pete."

"True, but if I keep them fed and treat their wounds, they're much less likely to make trouble."

"What about the militants?"

I laughed. "I'll be fine."

We both startled as the sound of gunfire drew close. I jumped to lock the back door and heard the pounding of running feet outside, followed by yelling, shots, and screams. My impulse was to rush out and check for any wounded, but I waited until everything grew still.

I stepped through the door into nearly total darkness. Coughing from the smoke, I pulled my shirt over my nose. A weak cry, more like a gasp, reached my ears. It emanated from an uncollected pile of trash, and I moved quickly through the shadows. Squeezing between two overflowing garbage cans, I peered down.

White-ringed eyes stared back from a thin, frightened face, and I could barely see the outline of a child. He wheezed, struggling to breathe. I picked him up, surprised he weighed so little, and hurried toward the clinic.

Blood spurted in geysers from his thigh as I ran. Safe inside the clinic, I felt within the hole, found the artery, and pinched it tight. Still holding the artery between my thumb and finger, I laid the child on a table.

"Hemostat!" I yelled. Laura brought a sterile kit and opened it beside me. "Pinch off the artery right above my fingers."

I eyed the kid, a skinny black boy probably less than eight years old. He writhed in pain as Laura probed the wound, but she managed to find and close the vessel. I let go of the bleeder gradually, trying to decide what job to tackle next. Examining him quickly, I found no other injuries.

"IV?" Laura asked.

I nodded, fighting back my growing panic. Breathing slowly, I washed my hands, gloved, and carefully spread out the suture kit. "Can you sedate him?"

"We have ether. What do you plan to do?"

"Either tie off or suture up that bleeder."

Laura frowned. "You know how?"

"Yeah. I've done it before."

Her eyes widened in surprise. "They taught you surgery?"

"No, I learned watching the surgeons, and it proved quite useful in the field."

Laura found ether and a mask, which she lowered slowly over the child's face. Once the ether was in place, I opened the wound farther to expose the artery. Using sterile gauze and saline, I cleaned the blood away and studied the bullet hole more closely. It'd come close to severing the femoral artery before it exited through his thigh. At least the artery looked clean enough to suture. I trimmed off the worst edges, chose a small curved needle, and used tiny stitches to reconnect the walls.

The kid started panting. "No more ether," I told Laura. She looked up as I opened the locked hemostat. There was some leakage, but the stitches all held tight, and the flowing blood brought color to his foot. I found an ankle pulse and smiled.

"He needs blood. That's why he's pantin'," I explained.

We both startled at a loud bang on the alley door.

"The supplies," Laura said.

I'd forgotten all about the militants. While she called our volunteers, I unlocked the door and let them outside to greet the truck. Returning to the kid, I noticed the clock hands stood near midnight.

Several armed men rushed inside. Pushing past me, they eyed the black families huddled in the front. Then they brought in crates of food, water, blankets—even diapers. Finally their leader spotted me. "You the doc?"

"Navy corpsman."

"Marine. Just got home." We shook hands, and he motioned for another man to bring me the medical supplies.

"This kid needs a hospital, ASAP. Can you take him?" I asked.

"Bullet wound?"

"Right through the artery. I sutured that, but he badly needs blood, and he may still have more injuries."

Another man, toting an M-14, marched in. He ignored me, studying the kid. "I'll put him in the back, ride with him," he said. Scowling at me, he ordered, "Bring the IV, boy."

I picked up the bottle and followed him outside where I saw more armed black men standing guard. They frowned at my presence but watched curiously as their guy gently placed the child on a blanket.

"I'll take that." The man grabbed the bottle from my hand. I climbed down, aware of the whites of many eyes gazing distrustfully at me.

"Thanks for bringin' the supplies and helpin' with the kid," I said. "All of us here are in your debt."

"Where you from, Whitey?" one guy asked.

"Tennessee."

He eyed me with a puzzled stare as I calmly turned and walked inside.

Chapter 10

L ocking the alley door behind me, I squinted in the light and glanced down. The child's blood covered my clothes from neck to shoes. Laura pointed toward the bathroom. As I passed through the crowd, they moved away, glancing at me with anxious eyes.

Inside the tiny bathroom, I locked the door, stripped to my shorts, and started washing. But my hands shook so hard I dropped the soap. I glanced into the mirror and gaped at the stranger staring back. Apart from all the blood, his eyes were dilated, crazy—a demon hiding in my soul. *You're still a coward,* he hissed. *Nothing you do will ever change that.* Closing the toilet, I sat down, head in hands.

I crouched, terrified and deafened by shrieking screams and bursts from semi-automatic weapons. My hands were streaked with other people's blood, drops running off my forehead, down my neck. I was wrist deep in blood inside someone else's body, and they were also screaming—still alive.

A flashlight in my teeth, I hunted in my kit and grabbed a metal hemostat, forcing it deep into the wound, feeling, finding, pinching off a torn vessel, and stopping the fountain of red blood. I locked the hemostat, sponged up the pool of blood, and gently pulled the artery up where I could see. The bullet had torn through one side. Without warning the hemostat slipped loose, shooting blood into my face. I heard Cole scream, saw the terror in his eyes.

Grabbing the hemostat, I pinched the flow again, this time a little farther from the hole. I cleaned the field as best I could, opened up a suture kit, and sewed the edges back together. Did Cole live?

I sat there for an hour before I finished washing. After rinsing out my clothing, I emerged, soaking wet, stepping gingerly between the startled families.

"Ya need clothes?" a grizzled black man whispered as I passed. I nodded, and he handed me a worn pair of shorts. "Take these."

"Thanks." Another man handed me a t-shirt. I went in the storage room, dried off and dressed in the borrowed clothes. They fit okay, and I felt a little calmer. Grabbing a blanket from the pile, I curled up. As I rolled on my side, I glimpsed Laura sleeping in the corner and realized she'd never gotten home.

* * *

Laura woke me before dawn. "There's an officer outside."

"What's he want?"

She shrugged, so I walked to the front and unlocked the door. I peered up at a burly, white-faced cop bleeding from his mouth and nose. Opening the door wider, I invited him inside. As I locked the door again, he leaned against the wall, taking in the crowd of refugees. They eyed him with distrust, scowling at the only two white men in their midst.

"What happened?" I asked, helping him into the back.

"They mobbed me...beat me bad." He sagged, and I lowered him onto the floor. He started shivering hard, and I handed him a blanket. "You a doctor?" he asked.

"No, but Laura is a nurse, and I'm a Navy corpsman." I helped him strip his shirt, seeing fresh welts made by something heavy. "Pipe?"

He nodded, wincing and pointing to his gut. I felt his pulse, and the weak, rapid rhythm suggested internal bleeding—maybe shock.

"You might need a surgeon."

"Call an ambulance?" He gasped, handing me his badge.

"Sure." When I couldn't get through on 911, I looked at his badge and called his precinct. "I'm at the free clinic up on Woodward. We have a Sergeant Steve Goodman here, beat pretty bad, probably has internal bleeding. Can you send an ambulance our way?"

"There aren't any left," the clerk said. "Can you bring him?"

"Don't have a car. Could you send a squad car?"

"Over there? You crazy? I'll talk to my Super and see what he can do."

Laura grabbed my arm and gestured to the cop, who now lay unconscious on the floor. Damn! She started an IV and O_2 while I kept an eye on his pulse and pressure, the former too high, the latter way too low.

"Bleeding?" she asked.

"Yeah, he's goin' into shock—probably has rib fractures and internal injuries. If they don't come soon, he could die."

I examined the man carefully, bandaged what I could, and made a complete list of his wounds. Laura kept a chart on his vitals and IV, but there was nothing more we knew to do. It took an hour for the ambulance to get there. We told them what we'd done, gave them our lists, and watched as they carted him away.

With the cop gone, tensions eased with the black folks. I retired to the back room, needing to relax. But as heat, fatigue, and hunger took their toll, an unprocessed terror took my mind.

"Pete?"

I flinched when Laura touched me.

She stepped back. "Are you okay?"

I shook my head, finding myself seated on the floor.

She brought me water, but I wasn't really there. V-C soldiers gathered all around me, one pointing an AK rifle at my face. Nearby their wounded screamed and bled. Grabbing my ears, I moaned, vaguely aware of other people crowding me, watching and whispering. Laura shooed them off, but I wasn't alone—Charlie had me!

When I found my way back, it was nearly noon. I moved slowly, unfolding my stiff body, feeling as sore as if I'd fought in a real battle. Pulling myself upright, I wrestled inner demons for control of my own mind. Laura finished serving lunch and offered me food, which I took without a word.

"Flashback?" she asked.

Still confused, it took me time to answer. "I guess."

"What caused it?"

I shrugged, still too focused on the past.

"Is that why you prefer to work construction?"

I'd never put those two thoughts together, but maybe Laura had a point. She didn't push the topic, just prepared for supper. By then I was able to help serve. As the sun finally disappeared into the sweltering dark, she asked, "You plan to stay?"

I listened to the sound of firearms outside and nodded. "You?"

She laid out our blankets in the storage room. Beyond tired, I lay down, expecting to sleep well. But lying on the concrete floor so close to Laura's body, seeing, hearing, smelling her not five feet away, consumed my mind. I'd not had a steady girlfriend since Emily, a nurse on the Sanctuary ship, and I desperately missed that physical intimacy.

At least my desire blocked the flashbacks. The memory remained, and I tried to analyze it, to separate the present from the past. Something about blood, the dying child, and the cop had jerked my awareness back in time. But no matter how I reasoned, I couldn't put a frame around the past. Exhaustion eventually dragged me into sleep.

"Pete?" Laura's voice jerked me out of bedlam.

I stood in a crouch, about to run. In the dark, I could just discern her face, the pallor of her skin, the whites of her eyes, and realized her forehead was wrinkled with concern, not fear. Thank God I hadn't hurt her.

"You were thrashing so much, I thought you might be in a nightmare. Want to talk?"

"Not really." Unable to make any sense out of my dreams, I lay back, now thoroughly awake. Laura stretched out and relaxed back into sleep. I watched her breasts rise and fall, smelled the sweat rising off her slender body. Eventually my fantasies of holding her close lured me into a different dream.

The next day we opened up for injured people only, having no more room for refugees. The black nationalists had brought us food for three days, but now we faced a toilet paper crisis. Since all the shops around were burnt, looted, or barred, we gathered scraps of paper, gauze, and cloth to fill the void. But we still got plenty of complaints.

The clinic had one bathroom, and with roughly fifty people, I had to unstop it several times a day. As the hours dragged by and the heat increased, tempers grew shorter, words harsher, faces grim. Some folks left, but the families mostly stayed, cowed by the fires and the guns.

Laura's face broadcast her fatigue, although she had slept more than me. My priorities were simple: food, water, sleep, and, above all else, avoiding flashbacks. By nightfall, Laura and I had both passed out. But sometime around midnight, I awoke to a loud, rumbling noise that made the building tremble like a mini earthquake—one that didn't go away. The noise came from out front, so I joined the families, peering through the narrow upper windows to the street.

"Are those tanks?" A preteen boy whispered.

I pushed close enough to see. The gleam of a streetlight reflected off a bayonet, a helmet. Soldiers marched between tanks as they rumbled down Woodward into the center of Detroit. I gaped. "The Army's here. They're occupyin' us."

Someone grabbed my shoulder, and I jerked. Recognizing Laura, I blocked my defensive moves and made room for her beside the window.

"Does that mean we're going home?" the boy asked, following me.

"Not yet. Most likely the fightin' will heat up."

The next day no one came to the clinic. The sounds of small arms and semi-automatic rifles continued to rattle on into the evening. The whoop of helicopter blades brought back more memories as the Army used choppers to keep snipers off the roofs.

Laura tallied up our remaining supplies and showed me the dwindling list. We exchanged a worried stare. No one knew how long this battle would continue or when anyone could bring us more supplies. As we lay down on our blankets that night— depressed, smelly, and totally exhausted—I rolled close enough to take Laura's hand. She held on. We fell asleep holding hands, and I woke to find her body nestled next to mine.

Afraid to move, I lay there, listening for rifles, tanks, and helicopter blades until I recognized what woke me—total silence. I waited, listening to nothing for an hour before I made my way out front. Several other people stood around, wide-awake.

"Is it over?" An older woman asked. "Who won?"

"I'd guess the Army."

The silence continued into morning. People opened the door, checking out the street. Slowly at first, but building like a flood, they poured outside and headed home to neighbors, relatives, or whoever could provide them food and shelter.

Laura and I tried to clean up the place, but that job brought us to our knees.

"Leave it," I said.

"I can't. It's our clinic!"

"Later. We'll come back tomorrow, or the next day—get some help. *I can't do it now!*"

Laura burst into tears. That surprised me—she'd been the strong one all along.

"Sorry," I whispered, wrapping an arm around her shoulders. She turned, burying her face against my chest. I held her close.

When we both calmed down, we ventured out, glancing up and down the empty street. The four days of destruction had left scars: broken windows, looted stores, and a car lying upside down on Woodward—burnt, wheels stripped. The desolation and silence felt surreal. Too exhausted to speak or even think, we walked home.

Chapter 11

I held my breath as we turned onto our street, but the riot had, for the most part, passed it by. My little car stood where I'd left it, untouched. The house looked the same. We spoke to neighbors venturing out after the siege and praised God for sparing us.

Vic smiled as we walked into the parlor. "You guys okay? Did the militants come, bring your supplies?"

"Yeah, thanks." I shook his hand. "How were things here?"

"Scary, especially when those rioters broke in. Luckily they didn't find anything worth taking."

"You okay?"

"Anna took good care of me." Vic winked and glanced at Laura. I glared back, but he just laughed.

Laura beat me to the shower. I went into my room and stripped down to my shorts. As soon as she came out, I stepped inside and luxuriated underneath gallons of hot water. Wrapped in a towel, I came out into the hall and saw Laura, hair still dripping, clad only in a robe. Securing the towel around my waist, I reached out and pulled her close. We exchanged a lingering kiss before I led her to my room.

The next day, Laura went back to nursing school, and I went to my construction job, but every time we passed, I found magic in her glance, her touch, the throaty sound of her words. I drew her in the nude, that special smile on her face, and then hid the picture where no one else would see. Thinking about her, which I did all the time, kept me from obsessing about my ugly past or my still uncertain future.

By the weekend, our house seemed almost back to normal. Madge and Lou returned together. Vic made an appointment to have his cast removed while Anna attended to his needs. Phil appeared on Saturday and cornered me in the dining room.

"Where's Ron? Have you seen him? Heard from him?"

Noting Phil's haggard face and reddened eyes, I spoke gently. "When did you last see him?"

Phil frowned. "We holed up in Hamtramck, smoked some weed, waiting for the riot to blow over. But on Wednesday, Ron went totally stir-crazy, said he needed something stronger. He left, and I haven't seen or heard from him since."

"You called around?"

As one of Anna's customers walked in, Phil pulled me into the parlor next to Vic. "I called the cops, the hospitals, the Red Cross and all our friends. He's never disappeared, not like this."

Vic pursed his lips. "What's he using?"

"Same as you, and he's not stupid," Phil snapped back.

"The hospitals are pretty overloaded. Maybe his paperwork got lost," I suggested.

Phil started pacing.

"We'll help," Vic promised, frowning at the floor.

Phil went up to his room, and Vic motioned me over. He told me to call all the morgues, but none of them reported a Ron Caro, or even a John Doe of his description. Vic seemed relieved, and I followed Phil upstairs.

Seeking out Laura, I asked, "You seen Ron?"

She shook her head. "Is he missing?"

"Since Wednesday."

She shrugged. "He probably got high and crashed somewhere."

I agreed with her assessment, but Phil kept searching, leaving our number everywhere he called. He looked panicked—like a parent seeking a lost child. Of course if it were Laura... I called the morgues again.

Around midnight the phone rang. Anna had attached a long cord to the phone and left it in the parlor next to Vic. He answered. I couldn't hear the words, but the tremor in his voice had me on my feet and pulling on my clothes. Running down the stairs, I asked, "They find Ron?"

Vic bit his lip hard and handed me the phone.

"Did you find Ron Caro?"

"Is he an olive-skinned male, mid-twenties, straight black hair, about five foot eight, one hundred sixty pounds?"

I stopped, my eyes meeting Vic's. "That could be him. What's he wearin'?"

"Jeans and a Rolling Stones t-shirt with a guitar design across the back."

I closed my eyes. "Yeah."

"Can you come to the morgue at DGH? It's in the basement."

Vic's eyes looked questioningly at me. I covered the mouthpiece and whispered, "Won't Phil go?"

Vic shook his head emphatically. "You go."

I would have said *Why me*, but the scowl on Vic's face silenced my complaint. "I'll be there soon." I placed the receiver in its cradle.

"You'll tell Phil?" I asked Vic.

"Only after you confirm it. He'll go nuts."

I raised an eyebrow, but I didn't doubt him. I'd seen guys crack up back in 'Nam—brave men who couldn't bear the loss of one more friend. It hurt me too. I bit my lip hard and refocused on the present.

The air outside felt like a sauna, still as death. As I drove down Woodward, the sliver of a moon rose above the towering buildings. The wide street looked deserted—too quiet, too few cars. I recalled nights in the bush, waiting in the silence, and found myself searching for an ambush.

Traffic thickened as I neared DGH and parked. Down the basement steps, I followed signs into the morgue. A sleepy officer sitting at the entrance raised his head as I walked in.

"Who ya here fer?"

"Someone called and said a John Doe matched the description of my missin' friend, Ron Caro?"

He searched through his records, nodded, and led me through another door. Rows of cots, each holding a full body bag, stood spaced like desks in a school classroom. The cop moved to Number 17 and unzipped it. I stepped back, gagging on the smell. His features were distorted by two days in the heat, but I felt certain it was Ron. Holding my breath and moving closer, I examined his fingers for the ring he always wore. I found it. Feeling sick, I turned away. The cop zipped up the bag and motioned me to follow.

The fresh air in the hallway revived me. I sat down, answering his questions as best I could. He didn't even blink when I gave Phil's name as "spouse." When he'd finished, I asked, "Cause of death?"

"Overdose. We found his body on Belle Isle with a hypo beside him. Looked like he shot up and fell asleep."

I walked outside in a dream, moving in slow motion when I wanted to be running. The still air shrouded me like a warm, damp blanket, making it difficult to breathe. I saw a pack of cop cars convening on an alley near my car. Hearing shots, I leaped into the Beetle and floored it. Racing out Grand River, I didn't slow down until I reached a quiet neighborhood. I pulled over, resting my head against the steering wheel, and took deep breaths to calm my nerves. I'd seen my share of death—too many corpses—but Ron's death was unexpected, unexplained, and wrong.

Reaching home, I found Phil waiting up with Vic, and as soon as I walked in, they read my face. "I'm so sorry," I whispered.

Vic's lips formed "thanks" behind Phil's sobbing body, and I nodded. Considering how difficult the trip had been for me, I understood why Phil couldn't go.

That weekend Ron's family arrived from Cincinnati to pick up his body and his personal effects. Phil stayed away as they breezed in and out, their disgust communicated in their wrinkled noses and averted, narrowed eyes. They drove off leaving only memories—no memorial scheduled, no funeral to attend. Safe inside my room, I pulled out my sketch of Ron and cried.

Phil hung around us like a zombie, all hope and motivation gone from his face. Vic's frown formed permanent wrinkles in his forehead. He kept Anna close—using her body as a balm for his distress.

Lou hid inside her room for a week. When she finally emerged, she said, "I've been snorting coke ever since they beat up Vic. Now I'm off to rehab." With that surprise announcement, she loaded all her stuff and left the house.

I found myself bouncing between heaven and hell. The time I spent with Laura was heaven, but during my alone times, especially at night, the nightmares and flashbacks took their toll.

I talked to Laura. "Let's leave, drive out to San Diego, or anywhere you want. Let's start in a safer place, get married."

She looked away. "I have another year of school."

"There are other nursing schools. You can transfer credits." But no matter how I argued it, Laura wouldn't listen. I finally realized she had no faith in me. Then I thought about driving west alone, working construction as I went. That had been my plan—before Laura. Fighting with myself, I didn't sleep at all until I finally faced the truth: I couldn't leave Laura here alone.

* * *

The next week an ambulance came to pick up Vic. I skipped work and followed. The X-rays of his broken leg looked good, and he was elated when they sawed off his cast. But as he looked down, his expression turned to horror. The skin oozed raw beneath the cast, and his leg had shrunk to little more than skin and bone. When he tried to stand, it barely held him.

"Shower twice a day and take Keflex for your skin. To muscle up your leg, you need P.T.," the surgeon said. "Come three times a week, and you'll be running in no time."

I raised an eyebrow at Vic, a silent offer of money, but he firmly shook his head. "I'll do P.T. on my own."

His hand cast came off next. Vic wiggled his fingers and grimaced. The doctor handed him a rubber ball. "Carry and squeeze this all the time. It helps to firm up the muscles, and you'll need to stretch the fingers too." He demonstrated. "You try."

Vic tried, but he could neither straighten his fingers nor tighten them around the ball. I read pain and frustration in his face. "Will it improve?" he asked the surgeon.

"If you come to P.T."

Vic touched his fingers lightly. "Should it hurt?"

The doctor reexamined the X-ray. "A couple of the bones are not completely healed. I could cast it again, but if you let it rest another week, that should help."

Vic nodded. After paying his bill, I wheeled him to my car. With help, he was able to sit in the front seat, and that small success made him smile.

Chapter 12

In late September, my construction job dried up, and I took a position as Orderly in the ER. It was pure "scut work," no chance to triage or suture, but I tried to make use of what I knew.

The nights were busier than I'd expected. After midnight, we got the refuse from the bars, usually cut up with broken bottles, sometimes knives. Next came the back-street abortions—young girls hemorrhaging or badly infected from coat hangers stuck inside their wombs. The auto and motorcycle accidents were worse, but at least we received the survivors, not the corpses. The injuries from car and motorcycle wrecks almost rivaled those made by Viet Cong explosives.

One night I watched as the ambulance crew brought in a ten-year-old black kid—all beat up. I stopped, observing closely. As the boy slouched in the wheelchair, he didn't cry or complain. He just stared into space, the only sign of suffering a deepening crease between his dark, glazed eyes.

I pulled up a chair, facing him. "I know where you're at, man. It's no fun. Why don't you leave that misery and join me?"

His eyes slowly focused on my face. "What ya want?"

I smiled. "That's better. Are you hurtin'?"

His eyes moved to his lower leg where I saw a fast-growing bruise. "Is it broke?" he asked, fear dilating his pupils.

"Don't worry, they can fix it. I've had broken bones before, and now they're good as new."

His face relaxed, eyes meeting mine. "What'd they do?"

"Well, first the doctor came and looked. Then he took a picture, which let him see inside, like Superman. And after seein' the picture, he put me to sleep while he fit all the pieces back together. When I woke up, my arm was wrapped up in a cast, and then it took a few more weeks to heal."

He almost smiled, so I pressed further. "What's your name?"

"Benny."

"Well, Benny, I've got work to do, but the doctor's comin', and in a few more weeks, you'll be up walkin'." As I stood, I collided with the ER doc. We both made our excuses as I left.

I felt good about that interaction. At the end of my shift, I asked the nurse about Benny.

"They put a cast on his leg and sent him home," she said.

"Home?" I couldn't contain the anger in my voice. "Who do you think hurt him?"

She stepped back. "There's no proof."

"You need proof?"

"Yeah, at least until the laws change. We can't even hold 'em overnight."

I clenched my fists. Walking outside, I passed an older black guy I'd seen cleaning floors. He sat on a low brick wall, smoking. As I passed, his eyes followed, studying my face.

"How's it going?" he asked.

"Not so good. I'm pissed."

"What about?"

"Benny, the kid who came in earlier—beat all to hell, broken leg?"

The man nodded. "Get's to you, don't it?" His eyes held mine.

I glared. "They sent him home."

He sighed and shook his head, stubbing the cigarette into the brick wall. "They say God watches over li'l children. I would like to think that's true."

I took a deep breath and said a prayer, wishing I could do something more substantial. Was this how Jake felt, sending me home? "Sometimes God helps, but changin' his family could take time," I finally said.

The black man nodded, dark eyes meeting mine. "Just 'member one thing, son. You ain't God." He stood up and headed back to work.

The next day, I couldn't sleep. I kept seeing Benny—his leg, his face. Suddenly I was back in 'Nam working on a boy, a boy I couldn't—or maybe shouldn't—heal. I woke up screaming.

Laura appeared and sat down on the bed. "What's wrong Pete?"

Her presence cleared my head. "Sorry, bad dream."

"You remember it?" She cuddled next to me.

At any other time, I'd have switched gears and paid attention just to her. But my mind was too stuck. "I'm in 'Nam."

"You're actually in Detroit. Would you rather be in 'Nam?"

I rolled over, knowing she would never understand.

Laura started rubbing my shoulders, working her way down my back. Her touch sent electric signals to my brain, waking sleeping hormones until it was impossible to focus on the dead. I turned and pulled her body against mine, smooth skin against my hairy chest, soft breasts against my muscles. She lifted her leg and I slid deep inside, tasting the sweetest drug of all.

In spite of Laura's TLC, my nightmares recurred. The next night I saw Ron, but his disfigured face was on someone else's body—throat cut wide. I woke on my feet, stumbling to the door.

The sun wasn't up yet, but when I reached the parlor, Vic was already on the phone. He stopped talking when he saw me, made excuses, and hung up.

I grabbed a cup of coffee and sank into a chair, my mind still grappling with the past.

"Where you at, Tennessee, back in 'Nam?" Vic used his walker to gimp over to my chair.

I nodded, setting down the cup before I spilled my coffee. I tried to quiet the trembling in my hands by clasping them tight behind my neck.

"You yelled out Rog'!' Were you with him?" Vic asked, pulling his chair up beside me.

"Oh my God!" I doubled over, forehead pressed against the table.

"Good guy?"

I tried to nod. "They split his throat open…a machete."

"You found him?"

"Fell over him…runnin' into camp."

"Alone?"

I hit my head against the table.

Vic placed his hand on my arm, and his touch reassured me. "Why were you alone? You run away?"

"No! I helped Cole, but they came."

"The Viet-Cong?"

"Gook's pointin' his gun right at my head!"

"What happened?"

"I don't know!" I struck my head again, and Vic put his arm around me, holding me against him while I sobbed.

Laura joined us, but even with her there, I couldn't pull myself together. She sat hugging me while I held on. Vic retreated to his sofa, but when Laura left for classes, he returned.

"Listen up, Tennessee. You can't stop remembering, but you can stop beating on yourself. Whatever shit happened doesn't make you a bad person. In war people die, some of them better folks than either you or me. But you're alive and home. Try looking forward."

I paid attention, knowing Vic had lived his whole life in a war zone, but I couldn't look ahead. How do you build on a past you can't remember?

"I keep seein' all these gross, disgustin' scenes. Drives me crazy, but I think it's forward progress—of sorts. Give me another year, and maybe I'll be ready."

Vic sighed. "You need a different job. Want to work for me?"

I glanced at his face and realized he was serious. "You still want me?"

"You're no crazier than anybody else, and you're honest—a rare virtue in this trade. The job has its risks, but I promise you'll see more mangled bodies in the ER than you will pushing drugs."

"Are you still sellin' heroin?"

He nodded.

I shook my head.

Vic raised an eyebrow. "You want to sell the pharmaceuticals? You'd need to study first—learn all about each medicine, what it's used for and the side effects. I've got books that you can read."

That offer was tempting, but illegal. It could lead to my arrest, and that might uncover a more serious charge—like murder. "Thanks, but I'll get another job."

Vic shrugged.

I found one in the brickyard stacking bricks. The work was exhausting, even in the cold. I came home aching head to foot—but I slept. For several weeks, I didn't do a thing but work, eat and sleep. Vic and Laura gave me puzzled stares and took turns suggesting other options. I ignored them. Every day I showed up at my job, took two bricks in each hand and moved them to a stack, again and again and again for eight long hours.

It occurred to me one evening that I'd become my pa. He'd worked manual labor all his life—hard jobs, long hours. Ma had said that was the only way he slept, and now I completely understood. By the end of a month, my muscles adapted, my brain cleared, and I rejoined the human race.

Laura saw the change and returned to sleep with me. I happily took the time to please her. As the winter settled in, we slept together any night she wasn't working. I'd never suffered through a Michigan winter. In Tennessee, it snowed maybe three times in a year, and the snow only lasted a few days. But here the snows piled up, melted, and refroze, icing the streets like rutted skating rinks.

The cold dark evenings led to long discussions. I learned Vic was one of a new breed—a "black boss." He looked more white than black, but he wore that title proudly. "Used to be only white men made the deals, but since they jailed Hoffa, it's been a free-for-all. Now some of us can get on top."

"Hoffa dealt in drugs?"

"I never said that." Vic rolled his eyes.

We debated the morality of selling controlled drugs. I argued heroin was addictive, potentially lethal, and should only be administered under a doctor's care. Vic disagreed, pointing out that doctors couldn't tell how bad you hurt or which narcotics worked for you. Other street drugs, like pot, you couldn't get from a doctor. Although marijuana helped with pain and seizures, it still couldn't be prescribed.

Phil ignored our discussions, dragging around like a wounded animal. Vic kept him on the payroll, insisting Phil was a necessary asset. I thought it was loyalty or pity, but there was a lot I didn't know. In mid-December, Phil disappeared. Vic searched high and low, suspecting suicide, but Phil's body never surfaced.

"Maybe he left town?" I suggested.

Vic frowned deep but didn't share his fears. By now he was walking on his own, but he still carried his left hand in a sling, and I frequently caught him shooting up.

"Take the money you gave me and see a specialist," I said.

"Mind your own business," he snapped back. He'd acquired more skills with his right hand. He could feed himself, shave, and do his buttons, but he asked me to write letters. I improved on his grammar, and after a while he didn't bother reading—just signed off.

Sometime before dawn on Groundhog Day, with the temperature outside colder than Alaska, Vic burst into my room. "Wake up, Tennessee. We got a serious problem."

"What?" I pulled myself upright rubbing sleep from my eyes. Laura wasn't there—working nights again—and my dreams had been wandering and intense.

"There's a warrant out for your arrest—for murder."

"Shit!" My heart skipped a beat. "Who'd you tell?"

Vic glared at me but slowly dropped his gaze. "Phil." He met my eyes, squinting in concern. "Phil's rough around the edges, but he's loyal. He wouldn't have squealed—unless…"

I studied Vic's face, uncertain what he meant but trusting him to come up with a plan. My own plan was to run as fast and far as possible. As *'coward'* hissed inside my head, I sprang to my feet and started pacing.

"Just turn yourself in," Vic said, following me closely. "I can get you out, and you won't look as guilty. Tell them it's a simple misunderstanding you expect your lawyer to sort out."

"You got a lawyer?" I turned and met his gaze.

Vic smiled. "Yeah, no problem. Just don't say a word about what happened. Understand?"

"What should I do—lie?"

"No!" Vic rolled his eyes. "You're a pitiful liar." My eyes widened in surprise, and he calmly explained. "Keep your mouth shut. My lawyer will arrange your bail, and I'll have you out by afternoon."

I hesitated, considering his plan. But this was Detroit, not Tennessee, and the cops here had a terrible reputation. I'd never even been in jail before.

Vic read my resistance and softened his approach. "If you just keep your cool, you'll be fine."

"Who's your lawyer?"

"Abe Morris."

"The Black Panther's lawyer? Are you crazy?"

Vic winced as if my words wounded him. "Abe is probably the best defense lawyer in the State. Get yourself dressed, and leave the legal shit to me."

I showered, a sick feeling in my gut. Vic saw himself as my protector, but I'd be stuck in a holding cell downtown, dealing with a random group of thugs. At breakfast, I couldn't eat a bite.

Vic drove me to the nearest police precinct. "Got your line down?" he asked.

"My lawyer, Abe Morris, has advised me not to talk unless he's present," I quoted.

Vic nodded. "Just stick to that line, and everything will be okay. I'll see you before supper."

I searched his face, knowing Vic lied all too well, but his eyes showed real compassion, and that calmed me. At the desk, I gave the officer my name. "There's a warrant out for my arrest. I want to clear up this confusion ASAP, so I'm turning myself in."

The cop looked up in surprise, checked the warrants, and nodded to the jailor, who led me to the back. They strip-searched me, kept my wallet and keys, and allowed me to dress in my street clothes again before pushing me into the holding cell.

"We'll be transporting you guys at three p.m.," the guard addressed a group of black men on my left. The heavy steel door clicked shut behind me.

Chapter 13

Finding a corner in the cell, I sat down, aware of the other prisoners staring pointedly. I didn't engage them but peeled a splinter off the bench and started cleaning my nails. The largest black man approached, looming over me. I squinted up at him. "What you want?"

"Why ya here, boy?" He prodded my leg with his boot.

"Murder."

His eyebrows rose as he glanced back at his buddies. "This Whitey's a murderer. What ya think of that?"

"I'm accused," I snapped. "Not guilty."

He reacted with a smile, revealing clean, white teeth. "Ya got an attitude, boy. They don't like that in prison. I think ya need an attitude adjustment."

I stood up slowly, studying my opponent. The man in my face was several inches taller, but he lacked Marine discipline and muscle.

"I'm at a disadvantage," I said softly. "I could kill you—easy—but then I would actually be a murderer." I narrowed my eyes, watching his as a flicker of concern passed through their depths.

"Where ya get all those muscles, boy?" he asked.

"Camp Pendleton, Da Nang, Hue."

He took a step back, his smile fading. "A Marine?"

"I trained with them for six months, served with them for a year."

"How many men ya kill?"

I shrugged.

One of his friends drew close. "You can take him, Spook. I think he's bluffing."

But Spook had a better close-up of my eyes. He shook his head. "I ain't fighting no Marine."

I didn't let my guard down, well aware that Spook might offer safety in one breath and strike before he drew the next. I waited until he took a seat and silently cased his gang for volunteers. No one moved. Satisfied, I went back to my corner.

A couple hours later, the cell door opened. I looked up.

"Pete Martin," the jailor called out.

I stood, feeling relief.

"Come over and hold out both your hands."

He cuffed me and pulled me down a long corridor into a large, high-ceilinged room. After pushing me into a chair, he left. I eyed a pair of ugly cops.

"We have questions," the fat one said. "And all you have to do is tell the truth."

"My lawyer, Abe Morris, advised me not to talk unless he's present."

The skinny cop played with his baton. "He ain't invited to this meeting, and you will talk. Understand?"

My thoughts jumped to broken fingers, Vic's beating, and Pa's memories from the POW camp, but I tried to keep my face expressionless.

"Where did you work?" The fat cop asked.

"When?"

"Last June."

"Construction for the new hospital wing."

"Did you know Vic Dumont?"

"Yes."

"Were you working there the day he got beat up?"

"Yes."

"Did you see the beating?"

"No." My head rang like a bell as the skinny cop struck me with his stick.

"What the fuck!" I reached my cuffed hands up to rub my head. "I told the truth."

"Wrong answer. Try again. Did you see the beating?"

"No." I yelped as he hit my head again. I was bleeding now—and furious. "You keep hittin' me, and nothin' you say will stand in court."

The cops conferred, and the fat one nodded. He whispered to his buddy, "Go get Angel."

The baton-wielding man left the room. I waited, wiping away a steady trickle of red blood. Soon a small man, carrying a metal box, entered. He set it on a chair and plugged it in.

"What's that?"

"You'll find out." He turned to the other two cops. "Cuff his feet."

I prepared to resist, but the fat cop hooked a rope between my handcuffs and next thing I knew, I was hanging from the ceiling. With no point of support, my kicks lacked any power. They caught and cuffed my ankles, attaching them to a chain lodged in the floor.

"Put the belt on," Angel said.

My eyes popped wide as they lifted my shirt and fastened a metal-studded belt around my waist. When Angel ran wires from the black box to the belt, I nearly panicked.

"What you doin'?" I yelled.

"These men will ask you questions, and if you answer right, I won't do a damn thing. But if you answer wrong, you get shocked. And I warn you—you won't like it."

I'd had some training about torture, about survival in a POW camp. But this was Detroit, USA. "You can't get away with this!"

"It all boils down to your word against mine, a confessed murderer against a trusted cop." Angel smiled knowingly as he stroked the box.

"Did you see the beating?" the fat cop asked again.

"No." The shock sucker-punched me so hard I couldn't scream, couldn't breathe. My body jerked like a fish caught on a line. When the pain eased, I felt warm pee run down my leg.

"Did you see the beating?"

"No." I jerked like a dying man—in so much pain I tried to scream, but couldn't.

When the worst had passed, the fat cop asked again, "Did you see the beating?"

"No!" The intense pain made my heart seize in my chest, and for a minute, I thought for sure I'd die. As the cramps and jerks receded, I thanked God to be alive. But when I tried moving my legs, they barely twitched.

Without further questioning, Angel turned a knob, and the next shock was so painful I passed out. When I came around, he repeated that performance—again, and again, and again.

Someone knocked. The skinny cop cracked the door open, whispered with someone, and slammed it shut again. "They're here for him." He nodded at my dangling body.

The two cops unhooked me and draped me in the chair where they stripped off the belt and ankle cuffs. Propping the door open, they dragged me down the hall and dropped me on the holding cell floor. I prayed Spook and his gang wouldn't take advantage, but they immediately lifted and placed me on the bench. Unable to control my quivering muscles, I lay waiting.

"It hurts less if ya don't try to move." Spook said.

I barely nodded, gradually aware that the men's grim expressions were directed at the coppers, not at me. As my muscles stopped jerking, I managed a deep breath. I tried to pull myself upright, but shooting pains made me grunt, and I leaned heavily against the wall. One man offered water. I drank it greedily and gagged.

"What's in this?"

"Pain meds—drink it down." Spook steadied the bottle in my hand. "Ya meet Angel?"

"That bitch!" I spit the word.

Spook smiled. "I'm beginning to respect your attitude. Ya give him what he wanted?"

I barely shook my head as unwanted tears slid down my face. I wiped them and instantly regretted the quick movement as my muscles cramped again.

"Don't feel bad. I cried like a baby when they were done with me." Spook touched my head. "Idiots left a scar."

The cell door opened, and the jailor motioned to me. I struggled to stand, muscles sluggish to respond. Spook helped me to the door, and the jailor helped me to the front. I almost made it to the desk when my legs totally gave out, and I fell hard.

Vic's eyes bulged wide when he saw me. "What the fuck?" He grabbed the desk cop by his collar.

The cop pushed Vic away. "You wanna get arrested?"

Vic glared at the cop and knelt beside me. "You hurt bad?"

"Get me outta here," I whispered.

He put his right arm around me, half-dragging me outside. Inside his car, I leaned back and closed my eyes. It felt like every nerve, from my busted head down to my feet, was on fire.

Vic checked the head wound. "I'll take you to the clinic."

I focused on slowing my breathing as he drove. Once there, Vic helped me through the door and to a bench. He called Dr. Su, who arrived shortly. The doctor's eyes grew wide when he walked in.

"Pete! What happen?"

"Police. Hit me, strung me up, belt . . ." I touched my waist.

Dr. Su pulled up my shirt. "You have burn. Electric?"

I nodded and pointed to my ankles. Dr. Su examined them as well, muttering what sounded like curses in Korean. "When they shock you, what happen?"

Just remembering made my muscles cramp so bad I couldn't speak. Finally I managed a few words. "Couldn't breathe… jerked…hurt!"

Dr. Su pulled out a camera and began taking pictures of my head, waist, and ankles. Next he took my pulse and pressure, making notes. "Rhythm okay," he said. "But pulse high and pressure dropping. I give you some prednisone to keep your pressure steady. Arrhythmia is most serious risk."

He searched the storeroom and brought out a syringe, which he stuck into my arm. Then he started with my face and worked his way down to my feet, testing sensation, movement, strength, and reflexes. "Can you stand?" he asked.

I pushed myself upright on shaky legs. Vic moved closer, but Su motioned him away.

"Hurt?"

"*Yes.*"

"What kind of hurt?"

"Ache, burn, cramp…shootin' pain." My knees began to buckle, and I fell onto the bench. "May I sit?"

Dr. Su nodded as he wrote his findings down. Rising to his feet, he gathered up supplies and proceeded to wash, sew, and bandage up my head.

"You have nerve damage in legs, but they heal. For next few weeks, you need pain meds and stay quiet. It okay to walk, do normal task, but no run, no lift, and go very slow on stairs. Understand?"

"Yeah." I glanced at Vic, and he nodded.

"Take pain meds as need, and put ice on head injury and burns. Come back see me next week, sooner if you feel weak and dizzy."

Vic stayed quiet driving home. When we reached the house, he helped me climb the porch stairs, which I managed very slowly. Once inside, I collapsed onto the couch. He brought me a pain pill and a beer, cold from the fridge. I gulped them both and pressed the icy bottle against my throbbing head.

"I came as quickly as I could." Vic kept his voice low, but his eyes smoldered like hot coals.

"I know. Thanks." Pain shot through my legs, and I bit hard on my lip, eyes watering.

Vic looked ready to explode. I'd never seen him furious—not like this—but all I could think about was getting into bed. "Can you help?" I nodded toward the stairs.

He half-carried me up to my room.

Laura was asleep after working her night shift, but Vic must have told her I was hurt. By afternoon, she'd taken on the job of nursing me—bringing ice and managing my pills. To my surprise, she never asked why I'd been arrested, leaving me to wonder what Vic said.

The next few weeks I couldn't work at all. Laura brought the radio to keep me entertained, but the Tet offensive was top story in the news. I hated listening to it, but when they read the names, I couldn't tear myself away. Between the nightmares and the cramping, burning, and twitching in my legs, I was a wreck.

Laura upped my codeine dose until I finally slept. Since the narcotics eased my flashbacks and nightmares, I was truly tempted to continue. But I feared becoming an addict—like Ma. So after a couple more weeks, I tapered off. The next night, I felt like shit and couldn't sleep a wink. I made my way downstairs an hour before dawn and was surprised to find Vic sitting at the table.

"Did I wake you?" I asked.

He shook his head.

"You have a nightmare?"

Vic looked away and bit his lip. I noted the lines etched deeply in his face and sat beside him. After some time, he met my gaze.

"They did the same to me."

"The cops? They shocked you?"

He nodded. "Pretty much like you, but it went on and on and on. I'd passed out before the end." He clenched his fists, staring daggers at the floor.

"They do this often?"

"Yeah."

Now I understood why he shot up heroin. It also explained the widespread fear of police, the targeting of specific cops, and the violence that erupted when murdering cops walked free. "Why don't you tell the Feds?"

"I'm sure they know." He pulled a small bag of white powder from his pocket.

Before he could prepare it, I asked, "Does that shit help?"

Vic glanced over with a frown. "You still hurt?"

I shrugged. "It's some better—can't work."

"Stay off the hard stuff if you can. It helps, but it's only a temporary fix. You always need more, and eventually you either have to give it up—or die."

"Which one are you plannin'?"

"You don't know the half of it." He dropped his gaze to the table, looking sadder and older than I'd ever seen him.

"Why don't you find a doctor for your hand and get clean?"

His hazel eyes met mine. "Why don't you leave?"

"I plan to. You want to come?"

"I can't. I'm in so deep I'll never leave Detroit—not alive. But you should go soon. I can't protect you anymore."

"What about the murder charge?"

"I'll handle that. You handle your own shit."

Vic struggled to keep his features calm. But behind that strong façade, I glimpsed raw terror. I'd seen that look on the face of dying men, and seeing it on Vic's face frightened me.

"You can't help me." He answered my unspoken question. "Please, just try to save yourself."

Chapter 14

Winter fought a long, hard retreat, and April—a time in Tennessee for flowering dogwoods—brought us only freezing cold and rain. On a chilly Sunday evening, we were sitting in the parlor listening to the radio when we heard the news. Dr. Martin Luther King was dead—shot by a white man down in Memphis. It sent ripples through the house, through the city, through the nation.

"Is that how they treat black folks where you're from?" Vic confronted me over supper. "Shoot 'em down like dogs?"

My mind flashed back to the murder I once witnessed, and I frowned, unable to disagree completely. "Memphis is a tough town, like Detroit, and some folks are definitely that way. Not my family."

Vic relaxed, knowing I'd lived comfortably with Phil. "What makes them different?"

"Ma's from Minnesota. But I think the real difference is religion. Mamaw taught us early on that everyone is equal before God."

"You're a Christian?"

"Yes—Methodist. Do you believe in God?"

Vic shook his head. "Dr. King believed, and look where that got him. I don't think much of a God who can't protect me."

I mulled over his logic and remembered what Jake said. "You have to understand death isn't permanent; it's only a door into another way of being—probably somewhere better than Detroit." As I spoke those words, a door opened inside me, revealing a connection I'd feared lost. Seeing Jake's face made me smile.

Vic watched me intently, looking puzzled.

Laura burst into the house. "They're breaking windows and burning things—again." She ran to me, and I put my arm around her.

I turned to Vic. "Would Dr. King approve?"

"Probably not. He called for peaceful demonstrations. But people still died, and now they've killed him too. If something doesn't change soon, this whole country will explode into a full-scale revolution."

Laura sought my eyes. "Should we leave? I don't want to stay here through another riot."

I walked onto the porch and looked up and down the street. It seemed calm—no gunshots, no smoke. I came back in. "Let's wait a bit. If things get too rocky, then we'll go."

We sat up late listening to the news. President Johnson declared a national day of mourning.

"That's all? Pretty pitiful," Vic muttered.

"What should he have done?" I asked.

"Enforced the law. Four years ago, they passed a law making it illegal to treat a person different because of sex, race, or religion. Now he needs to show that he'll enforce it."

"What do you think?" I asked Anna, who had joined us.

"Does that mean they'll start protecting women?"

Vic turned, eyebrows arched. "You think women need protection?"

Anna rolled her eyes and ran upstairs.

The National Guard occupied Detroit. By evening Guardsmen stood back to back at every major cross street. I wasn't the only person who looked twice at their helmeted faces frozen in a stare, full battle dress, and semi-automatic rifles resting on tense shoulders with bayonets in place.

All the schools and businesses stayed closed, but the hospitals still required staff. As I drove Laura to her job at Harper Hospital, the neighborhood seemed calm. I watched her walk inside and drove away. Along Woodward I glimpsed sporadic looting, but most folks stayed home. It helped when black leaders spoke in praise of Dr. King, asking his admirers to honor his non-violent legacy.

That evening when I picked Laura up, she looked pale. "Some addicts broke into our pharmacy, threatened the staff, and stole the morphine. They even came up on our floor, carrying guns."

I held her quivering body close. "You're safe, and as soon as you graduate, I promise we're gonna leave Detroit."

* * *

Shortly after King's death, Phil returned. Vic was elated, but I harbored many doubts. Phil wouldn't talk to me, turning away when I came near. Laura stayed busy with classes, work, and studying for her licensing exam. I wanted to leave soon, hoping a change would stop my nightmares.

Those dreams finally drove me to the VA clinic where the admissions clerk checked out my discharge papers. "The wording doesn't specify any battle stress, so you aren't covered for that treatment," she explained.

"Why do you think I got a general discharge?"

"Sorry."

That pissed me off so bad I spent the whole day in my room, too cowardly to carry out the plans inside my head. Laura came home and found me there.

"What happened?"

I explained, sharing my anger and resentment. Laura asked around, found a good private shrink, and drove me to my first appointment. Dr. Freedman lived in a charming cottage just north of Detroit in Royal Oak. His office opened onto a back porch, which he'd enclosed to make a cozy waiting room. Once inside, Laura settled into a soft chair. Unable to sit quietly, I paced.

Finally the door into the doctor's office opened, and a short, gray-haired man appeared. He smiled up at me. "I am Dr. Freedman." He spoke with an accent I remembered from Saigon, probably French. "You must be Pete Martin?"

I nodded.

"Would you like to come inside?"

Following Dr. Freedman into his office, I tried to take a seat but immediately bounced up. Circling the room, I passed a row of antique shelves filled to overflowing with books, old and new. I stopped and studied titles.

"You like books?" the doctor asked.

I shrugged, but the neatly filed rows of well-read texts— most of them in English, but some in French or German—told me a lot about the man.

The doctor took his seat in a leather swivel chair and reached in the ashtray for his pipe. "May I smoke?"

"Sure." I turned from my perusal of multiple diplomas, performance awards, and military honors to examine his wrinkled face more closely. He was probably about my father's age, mid-fifties, with thin, graying hair and inquisitive brown eyes. He didn't seem frightened or upset or even rushed. Feeling somewhat safer, I sat.

"That's better, no? Can you tell me why you're here?" He lit his pipe.

My muscles tensed again, but I managed to say, "Nightmares, flashbacks, things I can't recall."

"You are a veteran?"

"Yeah, Vietnam. I served from '64 to '67, although I spent my first year in the States."

"Which service?"

"Navy. I'm a corpsman—served with the Marines."

Dr. Freedman smiled. "A worthwhile job that has saved many lives."

I frowned.

"But not all lives can be saved." His brown eyes peered over metal-framed glasses, reading me.

I sat, silent, wondering if he had any concept of the chaos I had suffered through and seen. He emptied his pipe, refilling and tamping it, before pulling up his sleeve.

My eyes widened at the tattooed number. "You were in a concentration camp?"

"Yes. I fought with the French forces and was captured by the Germans. But when they realized I was Jewish, they sent me to Buchenwald, then Auschwitz."

My eyebrows rose, and I scrutinized his face. "You survived. How?"

"I was strong enough to be of use."

"My pa was a POW in Malaysia. He almost died."

Dr. Freedman frowned, lighting and drawing on his pipe. "Does that still bother him?"

"Yeah. He gets triggered real easy and goes off—can be violent. He's not a bad person, but when I was a kid, he hit me all the time, even strangled and beat me. More recently, he broke my nose."

"Did he ever insult you?"

That question made me pause. "Of course. All the time. So did Ma."

"What did he say?"

I winced. Pa's words had hit harder than his fists. "He called me an idiot, a coward."

"Do you think you're a coward?"

I couldn't answer—part of me said yes, part said no. Finally I admitted, "It's confusin'."

His eyes softened. "We take the words of our fathers seriously, even when our own experience later contradicts them."

I studied his face, longing to say more but fearing he would think me insane. Dr. Freedman waited, puffing on his pipe, and the scent of tobacco filled the air. That reminded me how much Pa hated smoke, and maybe for that reason, I found it reassuring. I took a deep breath and plunged in.

"Sometimes I hear Pa's voice callin' me a coward, but it comes from inside my own head."

The doctor's face stayed calm. "What do you do?"

"It depends. Sometimes I tell it to shut up, or just ignore it, and other times I have to walk away."

"Do you ever become violent?"

I started to say no, until I remembered shooting the enforcer. "Only once…or twice."

He waited for more. When I didn't continue, he asked, "What set it off?"

"Someone beatin' up a friend."

"You stopped him?"

"Yeah."

"More than stopped him?"

"Yeah."

"Were you arrested?"

I winced and nodded once.

"Is any of that bothering you now?"

I thought back to the torture. It was painful, redefining my understanding of that word, and it totally changed my opinion of police. But I didn't have nightmares about Angel.

"No. My nightmares are always about 'Nam, my last mission."

The doctor set his pipe down and picked up his pen. "What do you recall about that mission?"

"Pieces and parts, but then I forget again. Can't ever remember it straight through."

"We'll work on that. What about your childhood? Are there parts of that you can't recall?"

I thought back to Memphis and all the disgusting stuff I told to Jake. "A friend talked me through it years ago. I think it's good."

"Okay. We'll start with your dreams—see where they lead. Tell me the first thing that happens in your dream."

I stared at the carpet, reliving the exhaustion…heat…fear. What was the first thing in my dream?

"Blood. I'm inside my buddy's chest, tryin' to pinch off an artery that's spurtin'."

I glanced at his face, but he simply said, "Go on."

"I get a hemostat on it, but I think—if that's all I do, he'll lose his arm. I'm drenched in his blood, and he's starin' right at me, terrified. Somehow I find a flashlight, hold it in my teeth, find sutures, and sew the edges back together."

"Did it work?"

"I guess." I stopped talking and chewed hard on my lip.

The doctor continued taking notes. But when I remained quiet, he raised his eyes. "What happened next?"

"That's where things get scary. I'm tryin' to help Cole, and I see him look behind me. I turn and this gook has his rifle in my face."

"What were you thinking when you saw him?"

"It's over." My gut cramped and my hands began to sweat.

"But you are still alive, so what happened?"

"I don't know!" My fists clenched.

Dr. Freedman kept writing. "We know he didn't shoot. Did someone shoot him?"

"No one's left!" A blurred image of bodies flashed before me.

"Did he want something? Your medical skills, perhaps?"

I choked at the sudden image of a boy, maybe a teenager, but tiny. "Yeah. That's right. They brought a kid. But he had a bullet in his brain."

"Was he dead?"

"No. They expected me to save him, but there was nothin' I could do." Feeling intense pressure, I pushed my hands against my temples.

Dr. Freedman peered over his glasses. "That is a serious dilemma. Your only hope for survival is a task, which appears, at first glance, to be impossible. What would you do now?"

His question fast-forwarded me into the present, providing a much-needed break. "I'd probably try to please them—buy more time."

"That makes sense. How would you do that?"

I wasn't sure if it was memory or logic, but I said, "Remove the bullet. Close the wound? That would damage the kid, but it might make them happy."

"A moral dilemma—save the kid, or save yourself? But the kid may be past saving, so you choose to save yourself. No?"

I cringed at the thought, my head close to exploding. How could I hurt a child—any child? My hands started shaking. "No! I couldn't!"

"Is that what you told them?"

I squeezed my head. But I could feel my fingers digging deep inside the boy's skull, removing the bullet and suturing the wound. The hissed word—*coward*—repeated in my brain until I finally leaped to my feet, fists clenched.

"What's happening?" the doctor asked.

I paced around the office, longing to escape. But Laura was waiting, and I couldn't act the coward. Taking a deeper breath, I forced myself to sit, but that did nothing for my guilt.

"I ruined any chance that poor kid had."

Dr. Freedman's eyes grew sad. "Those types of choices cause much suffering. In the camps, they'd ask parents to choose among their children, make them feel responsible for their child's death. Of course the Nazis killed them, but the parents, those who live, still suffer terribly from guilt."

"I could've died. I should've died. I love kids!" Furious with myself, I punched my head.

"That wouldn't have helped you or the boy. His life was over, and you knew it."

That was true. The bullet wound would putrefy—infect his brain, his bloodstream—and slowly, painfully, destroy him.

"You, on the other hand, had a chance to live."

All of a sudden, I remembered what Jake said: *When someone puts a loaded gun to your head, the rules change.* The pressure inside my head eased off, and I sighed.

The doctor looked up from his notes. "You made a connection?"

"Yeah, to what my friend told me back when I was ten. I felt bad about somethin' I did…when there was a gun held to my head."

His eyebrows rose. "Tell me."

I told him everything I'd said to Jake: my mother's rape, the ugly man holding me at gunpoint, how he made me suck him 'til I puked. "He shot his gun by my head, and my ear hurt, started bleedin'. I thought for sure he'd shot me!"

The doctor's eyes widened. "You must have identified strongly with that boy, given your experience was very much the same and you were, once again, at gunpoint. It must have felt as though that bullet went through your head, destroying your own brain—how terrifying!"

I peered into his eyes but found no sarcasm there, only concern and empathy. I recalled the black pianist they shot—his faceless corpse. It made no sense at all, considering the ugly deaths I'd seen in Vietnam, but a bullet through your brain, exploding out your face, still seemed the most disgusting way to die.

"Our time is up, but you made excellent progress. Can you come back tomorrow, same time?"

I agreed, grateful he hadn't put it off. I didn't expect to get much sleep.

Chapter 15

While Laura drove us home, I replayed the therapy session in my head. Dr. Freedman had managed to get inside my brain and help me understand what I'd previously thought crazy. Since I'd always identified with other injured kids, his reasoning made perfect sense to me.

Laura searched my face. "How'd it go?"

"It helped. The doctor's a survivor of the concentration camps. He understood—really understood."

She parked by the house and gave me a big hug. "That's super. When are you planning to go back?"

"Tomorrow. We still have a lot to talk about. Thanks for findin' him." I returned her hug with a lover's kiss.

"He came well recommended," she mumbled through the kiss.

Once inside, Laura led me to the kitchen. "Hungry?"

I nodded.

"What would you like?"

"Food."

She pulled out leftover ham and handed me three Idaho potatoes. I found a knife and started peeling.

"Have you seen Lou?" I asked.

Laura frowned. "Yeah, I visited last week. The rehab house is nice, but Lou seemed offish. I think she and Madge have talked a lot."

"Madge seems real independent. You think she's a role model for Lou?"

"Maybe." Laura added my potatoes to the stew and stirred. "Do you believe homosexuality's a sin?"

Puzzled by the topic shift, I glanced at Laura's face, but all I read there was confusion. "I don't know, maybe. It's not listed in the Ten Commandments."

"You think Ron went to heaven or to hell?"

I winced. "If God loves music, Ron's in heaven. That guy could croon to match the angels!" As tears stung my eyes, I turned away.

"You two were friends?"

"Yeah."

She frowned.

"Not like that!"

Laura sniffed. "Of course not, but I know it upset you when he died."

"He reminded me of Cole, one of my buddies back in 'Nam." I paused, thinking back. "Cole was like Ron in many ways—always kind."

"Is he still in Vietnam?"

"No, he died."

She stopped stirring and wrapped both arms around me. "That's got to hurt, losing all your friends."

I rested my head on hers, thinking about Cole. "They shot him. That's what happened. That's what I need to tell my shrink."

* * *

The next day, I hurried back to Dr. Freedman's office, sketchbook in hand. He arrived late and found me in the waiting room, pacing.

"Hello, Pete. Are you ready?"

I followed him inside and quickly took my chair. Wound tight as a tripwire, I opened my sketchbook to a picture of Cole gesturing and grinning as he talked about his girl.

"I remembered more about Cole."

Dr. Freedman studied the sketch carefully. Setting it aside, he lit his pipe. "Did this occur after you were captured?"

"Yeah. One of the gooks took the boy and hurried off. I thought they'd shoot me, but they brought another man. While I worked, I counted a dozen V-C soldiers. Then Cole cried out." I grimaced, realizing I'd forgotten to give morphine. Idiot!

"What happened?"

"They shot him—in the head."

"What did you do?"

"I don't know." I clenched my fists, filled with rage, self-disgust, and other emotions I couldn't even name. "I must've gone crazy."

"Why do you say that?"

"The Navy sent me home."

He puffed a minute on his pipe. "Let us not jump to our conclusions. Let us trace the facts as they unfold. You see them shoot Cole, but you also see a dozen enemy soldiers. What can you do?"

"Absolutely nothin'." I remembered staring at my gun, knowing I'd be dead before I grabbed it. "I was carin' for their wounded when a messenger arrived, and all the V-C got real excited. My guard turned around so he could hear them, and I ran."

"Good. Where did you run?"

"Across the camp toward our guards." I grabbed my head as another memory hit me. "I found Rog'. They'd slit his throat." I reached for the drawings and found a sketch of Rog'—laughing as if nothing could go wrong.

"A good friend?"

I nodded, my throat too tight to speak.

"Were there other survivors?"

I frowned and shrugged. "I heard explosions…" I stopped, confused, counting up the dead. "Six or seven of our guys must have died in that barrage—or shortly after. With Cole, both sentries, and me…" I flung up my hands, confusion winning.

"How many men in your platoon?"

"The attack was on our squad. We had twelve men."

"That leaves one or two men unaccounted for. How did you get back?"

"The other squads moved in, but by then I couldn't think straight. Afterwards, the chopper flew me to Da Nang, and their C.O. stuck me in the brig. The next day, our C.O. came and asked a million questions, but I was still in shock, couldn't tell him much." I paused, struggling with too much reality. "You think I'm the only one alive?"

"You could easily find out. All their deaths are public knowledge."

I had no idea what he said. Why was I here? Why me? There were better men—smarter, kinder, stronger, and married men with kids. I wanted them to live. Not me! Not me!

"Pete?"

His voice reached my ears from very far away, but I felt his hand touch mine and grabbed it, holding on.

"Pete, are you religious?"

I nodded.

"Do you think there is a reason we are here?"

"We're in hell?"

"Maybe. If so, why are we here?"

"We're sinners, murderers, hypocrites. We're lost."

"You think God took the good folks and left you behind because you sinned?"

I hesitated. "Yes."

"And what does He ask sinners to do?"

"Repent, ask forgiveness, and stop sinnin'."

"Do you want to try that?"

His words hit me like a bullet, and I broke down in tears. "Oh God, forgive me. Please forgive me!" I sobbed so hard I couldn't talk. The doctor kept my hand, holding me together while I screamed, "Oh Jesus. Please! Forgive me!"

* * *

I was grateful to come home and find the house deserted. Climbing upstairs to my room, I locked the door and curled up on the mattress. Could Jesus forgive me? I'd broken God's Commandments, every single one. I'd stopped even thinking about God, never prayed, and was totally immersed in my own life. I'd lied and cursed and even hit my pa. Sleeping with Laura was not adultery, but it wasn't a holy marriage either. And what about coveting my neighbor's property? I'd desired Laura when I knew she cared for Vic.

But those sins all paled next to killing. How many people? I didn't even know, but I knew some were barely in their teens. I should never have volunteered to go with the Marines. Only a fool would think he could save lives and never take one.

Eventually I slept, waking to the sound of voices floating up the stairs. My ears perked up when I heard Phil.

"It's the only way," Phil said. "I know they're left-wing and militant, but no other group is willing to support us. Without their backing, we're as good as dead."

"They won't accept Pete," Vic said.

"No, they won't. You gonna tell 'im?"

"Of course. You understand what you have to do?"

"Yeah. Don't worry, bro."

"Stay cool, and thanks."

I heard the front door close. I would have slept again except for worrying about Vic and whatever Phil had planned. Finally I got up, wandered to the bathroom, and then trotted down the stairs.

"Hey, Vic. Glad you're back." I noted the deep circles underneath his eyes, the wired stare. "Did I hear Phil?

"We thought you were sleeping, or he'd have said hello." Vic scrutinized my face. "You okay?"

I shrugged. "Saw this shrink and just talkin' wore me out. I caught a nap."

Vic's eyes brightened. "You're dealing with your shit? That's good."

"You should meet this guy. He's a survivor of Auschwitz, no less."

"I can't. We got a problem."

"About the murder?" My gut clenched.

Vic shook his head. "You recall the meeting here, last summer?"

"Sure."

"Phil did some digging and discovered they betrayed us, paid the cops to torture Ron—and Phil—and you." Fury burned in his eyes.

I glared back, feeling like I'd just been sucker-punched. When I could speak again, I asked, "Is Phil okay?"

"Yeah, but he's embarrassed—thinks he failed. I'm sure they'd have found you anyway. After the cops were done, the Panthers took him in, and now he's a member. I just hope they can protect him."

"And you?" I raised an eyebrow.

"You should think about yourself. You have to leave."

"What about the murder charge?"

"I took care of that."

My head jerked up, and I stared hard at Vic. "You confessed?"

He dropped his gaze. "I should've done it earlier. Truth is, I was scared—both of the dealer and the cops." He raised his eyes, holding mine in a sincere apology. "When I told the detective I shot in self-defense, he didn't even threaten to press charges. And even if he did, it would never get past the Grand Jury."

I sighed in relief. That murder had weighed heavy on my mind. "Laura graduates next week."

"Listen up!" Vic snapped. "You don't have another week."

I began to understand. "You're sayin' we're at a war?"

Vic nodded vigorously. "Starting right now, anything could happen."

I sat in silence, his reality slowly sinking in. "Okay. I'll leave today. But you better keep in touch."

"Same here."

We shook hands and grabbed shoulders. I ran upstairs, packed my rucksack, and tackled Laura's room—stuffing clothes into bags and books into boxes. Amazed at how much stuff she had, I dragged it all downstairs and stowed it safely in my car.

Done with packing, I paced, waiting impatiently for Laura to return. Vic stretched out on the sofa, muscles tense and jaws clenched against pain. I watched for a few minutes more, and when he didn't shoot up, I stayed alert.

The phone rang and Vic grabbed it. "Tennessee! RUN! NOW!"

I scrambled to my feet, expecting him to follow. But as I sprinted out the door, he pulled the M-14 from underneath the couch. Unclear about his plans, I ran faster. I jumped into my Beetle as a long black limo rounded the far corner and accelerated toward me.

Watching the limo in my mirror, I glimpsed the figure of a child. I rolled down my window and yelled, "Marcos. Go home! Run!"

He stared at me, the limo, and took off like a squirrel. I sped away as bullets hit my car. One splintered the rear windshield and embedded in the dashboard. I was fast approaching Woodward when Laura turned off it and drove past. Wildly I motioned her to follow. She managed a tight U-turn behind me. As I watched in my mirror, three white men with rifles jumped from the limo and ran into our house.

I hesitated, thinking about Vic, although I knew he and Phil had made a plan. But when I heard the rattle of semi-automatic weapons, I gunned my Beetle across rush-hour traffic, Laura's Chevy on my tail. We peeled left in front of cars, ignoring the din of honking horns and squealing brakes, and raced north as fast as we could drive.

By the time we reached the freeway, I was pretty sure no one had followed, but I kept right on going until we reached the country before pulling off for gas. Laura stopped behind me. Jumping from her car, she ran to me.

"What just happened?"

"Drug war, and I'm not sure Vic made it."

Her eyes widened, and she started trembling. I wrapped my free arm around her, torn between saving her and going back for Vic. But I feared it was too late to rescue him.

"Don't worry, sweets. We'll find a safer place."

"But I need my books, my clothes."

"I packed your room." I pointed to the bags and boxes in the backseat.

She stared at the shattered window, the glass shards covering her bags, and ran her worried eyes over me. "Are you…?"

"I'm fine." I walked around the car and opened up the hood, checking carefully for engine damage. Luckily most of the bullets hit the bumper. A few hit the left fender, and my left rear tire hissed—nearly flat.

Sighing, I pulled out the jack and spare. By the time I'd finished, Laura had found a broom and swept the broken glass off her stuff.

"Where to?" I asked.

"My parents' farm?"

That sounded like a plan. "Is it far?"

She glanced at her watch. "We should get there around dark; just follow me."

Chapter 16

If Laura hadn't led, I never would have found her family's farm. She wandered through a maze of twisty two-lanes, passing by small towns and farms with newly planted fields. We arrived well past dark, almost midnight, crunching up a long gravel drive.

The night was clear with a full moon, which allowed me to see the ghostly image of a farmhouse squatting like a mushroom in the middle of a field. The land lay almost flat, stripped of trees, except for a few big oaks for shading the southwest. Past the house stood a barn and several sheds, and beyond the barn lay pastures bordered with wire fences stretching straight as railroad tracks out to the horizon.

Laura headed for the door while I grabbed her bags. The door opened, and a large man, dressed only in shorts and carrying a shotgun, stepped outside.

"Who's there?"

"Hi Dad, it's me and a friend!" Laura yelled, undaunted by the shotgun pointed at her.

A small woman in a nightgown joined the man. "Calm down, Donald, it's Laura with a friend."

I'd set down the bags and grabbed my sidearm, but when her pa lowered his shotgun, I returned mine to its holster. Picking up her bags again, I followed to the porch.

Laura made the introductions. I put down the bags and shook her father's hand, surprised by the vicious tightness of his grip and the paranoia in his eyes.

"Pleased to meet you, Mr. Davenport," I said. He merely grunted.

"Hi Pete. I'm Martha, Laura's mom." The short, round-faced woman spoke kindly, as if making up for her husband's cool reception. "Would you like something to eat? We have all sorts of snacks and cookies in the kitchen, or if you prefer, I'll make a sandwich. Laura said you drove straight through and didn't stop for supper. You must be tired. I'm thinking you could sleep on the sofa in the study, if you don't mind sleeping on a sofa. We don't have an extra bed, but I can make up the sofa like a bed." She stopped for breath.

I raised an eyebrow at Laura. She cocked her head and shrugged. Smiling at her ma, I said. "A sandwich sounds real good."

Donald grabbed Laura's bags and headed up the stairs with Laura following. I went out to get my rucksack. By the time I'd returned and found the study, Martha was transforming the couch into a bed.

"Why don't you look in the fridge and find something you like? We have ham or turkey, or some leftover hamburgers I could heat for you."

The kitchen, a sizeable room with a round dining table, immediately reminded me of home. As I rummaged through the fridge, Martha followed, laying out two plates, napkins, and silverware.

Laura quickly joined us. "Sandwiches?"

I held up ham and cheese.

"I have fresh tomatoes," Martha added, slicing one before I even spoke. "Would you like onions or fresh lettuce?"

"No thanks, but tomatoes would be great."

Laura added those slices to the sandwiches she made, and we took our seats at the table. Martha hovered over us.

"You'll find fresh cookies in the cookie jar, but if you prefer, I have an apple pie. It's in the freezer. Should I get it? I made it last week, but my neighbor—Mrs. Rubenstein—she never came. Said she had a fever, although you never know, she might have needed an excuse. I don't think she gets out much. They have a son, and he's retarded, so maybe she'd rather stay at home."

"Cookies are fine," I said.

Laura started laughing, hiding her mouth behind a napkin. And after the excesses of my day—the grueling therapy, close escape from gunmen, fears for Vic's life, and lengthy drive— Martha's rambling story struck me silly. I joined Laura, giggling like a kid.

Martha turned to go, explaining over her shoulder, "Donald and I always get up at dawn so he can eat breakfast before milking. If you have everything you need, I'm off to bed."

"'Night, Mom. Sleep well," Laura managed between snorts.

I listened for her footsteps on the stairs. "Hope I didn't insult her," I whispered, wiping mayonnaise and mustard off my face.

Laura winked. "I'm so used to her talking all the time, sometimes I forget how ridiculous it sounds. At least you were trying to be nice." She kept giggling until I finally hugged her, kissing her on her messy mouth. She kissed me back, and I relaxed. Laura calmed me better than a drug.

After we ate, Laura went upstairs to sleep, and I tossed and turned on the narrow couch. My mind ran laps inside my head as I worried about Vic, Marcos, my own future, and where I wanted to go next. I didn't sleep until the moon had set, and then I awoke right after dawn. Taking time to shower, shave, and dress, I walked onto the back porch and surveyed the acreage. Except for a small orchard on a rise behind the house, the entire place was in grass.

Martha joined me, coffee cup in hand.

"How much of this is yours?" I asked.

"One hundred twenty acres. The original farm was a section, six hundred forty acres and a mile square, but it's been divided every generation, and this is the largest parcel left. When my parents died, I inherited the place, and Donald needed a job after the war. So this is where we've lived for all those years."

Her story rang familiar. "Where I grew up, it's hilly, and the farms are much smaller. Ours is only forty acres, but it's been in Pa's family for at least a hundred years."

"You grew up on a farm?" She looked at me with sudden interest.

"Kind of. Pa didn't farm it, so it's mostly in big trees with a large creek and lots of catfish."

"Sounds pretty. You want breakfast?"

I followed Martha inside, ignoring all her gossip about unfamiliar folks. She fried eggs and ham and poured me juice. Pulling up a chair, she grew quiet, allowing me to eat before she asked, "Is Laura done with nursing school?"

I sighed. "Not quite. Things got so dangerous; we really had to leave. I don't know the details, but I think she's very close to finishin'."

Martha pursed her lips.

After breakfast, I followed the worn footpath to the barn into the cool shadow of the milking station. I watched Donald washing the cows' udders and putting suction cups over their teats. The stanchions were spotless, which truly impressed me after my experience cleaning stalls with Jake.

"That's a lot of work twice a day, every day." I spoke loudly, suspecting Laura's father might be deaf. "You keep it amazingly clean."

Donald grinned. "Cleanest barn in the state. I've got the paperwork to prove it. You grow up on a farm?"

"Yes and no. We lived on a farm, but Pa worked other jobs. Right now all we raise are garden crops."

"What's your job?"

"I'm between jobs." I knew that wouldn't sit well, and his glare confirmed it.

Laura climbed down from the hayloft, brushing the dried grass from her clothes. She must've woke up with her parents and was helping feed the cows.

"Pete was in Vietnam last year," she told her pa.

Donald's glare softened. "Which service?"

"Navy corpsman," I said.

He eyed me up and down as if judging a prize bull. "Laura tell you that I served in World War II?"

I nodded. "Infantry—a long, tough slog across Europe. But you won."

"We'll win in Vietnam. You wait and see." He narrowed his eyes, daring me to argue.

"I hope so." The news from the front was more ominous each day, and the stateside support grew more divided.

Donald's jaw clenched tight.

"Tell him all about our cows." Laura shot me a warning glance.

"Well, these are dairy cows, a mix of Guernsey and Holstein. The Guernseys produce the best cream, but the Holsteins produce the most milk. Mine do both."

He went on to explain the genetics behind breeding, how he chose his cattle, and thoroughly described every cow in the herd. Laura had obviously picked his favorite topic, and I listened closely. He was intelligent, obsessive, defensive, and probably could get violent when crossed— just like Pa.

Having educated me, Donald went into the dairy room to wash, and Laura offered a tour of the remaining farm. In the orchard, the apple and cherry trees had budded. A dozen chickens were scratching in the dirt beneath the trees, so we entered the henhouse and gathered up their eggs, stacking them carefully in a bucket. After carrying all the eggs into the kitchen, Laura took me to an old shed off the barn.

"This is Beauty." She smoothed the silky black coat on a medium-sized mare. "She's a Tennessee walker, shipped here as a filly from somewhere south of Nashville almost fifteen years ago. Can you ride?"

I shook my head. Horses were a luxury I'd never enjoyed.

"Want to try?"

I shrugged.

She haltered the mare and led her out into the sunshine. "Climb up on that stile."

I followed her eyes to a step near the fence and climbed up. She led the horse beside me, and I jumped aboard, grabbing the mane. The horse quivered, then bumped along, and suddenly settled into a smoother gait. Laura ran beside us, leading Beauty.

"Like it?"

"Yeah!" I loved the feeling of moving with the horse, gliding without effort across the grassy field. Laura continued to run alongside until she slowed down, out of breath.

"You want to ride?" I asked.

She grinned as I slid to the ground. Still holding the lead line, she grabbed the horse's mane, leaped up, and threw her leg across the mare's broad back. Almost without warning, she and the horse took off, running full out across the field. I held my breath as I watched. Slowing they circled and walked quickly back toward me.

"Can I do that?"

"Not without practice." She patted Beauty on the neck. "I love to ride."

I walked beside them to the barn, grateful for this chance to watch Laura with her family and especially with her horse.

Who'd have guessed she could ride like a wild Indian? We returned to help her pa scrub down the milking parlor. As we finished up, Martha rang the bell for dinner, which consisted of enough food to feed a whole platoon.

After eating, Donald retreated to his room. Martha started the dishes, shooing us from the kitchen, and Laura pulled me outside to the porch. We sat, well fed and quiet, on a bench shaded by oaks. Finally she said, "I called the nursing school and explained about the shooting. They said I'd completed everything essential, and they'll send my diploma in the mail."

I watched her face as she stared sadly at the floor. Gradually I realized what she hadn't dared to say. My heart sank. "You're stayin'?"

Laura sighed deeply, lifting green eyes filled with regret. "I discussed this with Mom, and she wants me to stay. Dad can be hateful, and he's better with me here. Maybe once you settle, get a real job…"

I winced, turning away.

"That's not what I meant." She took my hands. "I want us to stay in touch, call, write, but I have unfinished business with my folks." She hesitated, drawing a deep breath, and went on. "You realize my life here was not a box of chocolates?"

I squeezed both her hands. "Then why stay?"

"I can't keep running from my past. You have unfinished business too—with your folks and remembering about 'Nam. You need to find another therapist and figure out what really happened there. When we're both ready, we can move somewhere together."

I couldn't answer, my tongue frozen in my mouth.

She read my face and frowned. "I love you, Pete! But I can't stand by and see you waste your life moving bricks from one pile to the other." Laura took my downcast face between her hands. "You're kinder and more talented than anyone I know. Don't throw that away. From what you've told me, you should've died in Vietnam. God spared you, and He must have had a reason. If He believes in you, and I believe in you, why can't you believe in yourself?"

'Cause I'm a fuckin' coward! But I didn't say a word. Why would such a beautiful, educated woman run off with a crazy guy like me? Fighting back anger and desire, I tried to steady the tremor in my voice.

"Are you gonna be safe here with your pa?"

Laura shrugged. "He's fine unless he's triggered, and I pretty much know what not to say."

I understood that logic all too well.

"Where will you go?" she asked.

"Right now? I guess back home, see how things are goin' with my folks."

Laura raised an eyebrow, glancing at my nose.

"I'll probably stay with my buddy at UT."

She nodded. "Give me his phone number and address. I'll give you mine."

I hugged her, sniffing the sweet scent of her hair. "You know I love you," I whispered in her ear.

Tears sprang into her eyes. "I'll miss you too, lover." Then she kissed me in a way that left me breathless.

While Laura went inside and copied down our numbers, I unloaded her remaining boxes from the car. I carried those inside and repacked my rucksack before saying thank you to her folks. After giving Laura one long, last embrace, I finally hit the road—back to Detroit.

Chapter 17

By the time I reached the city, I'd decided on a plan. My first stop was the bank, to withdraw traveling funds. To my horror, I found my balance disappeared, and I only had five hundred dollars left. That was roughly the amount Vic had stolen. I asked to see the last withdrawal slip, and the signature was my name, but the handwriting matched Vic's awkward scrawl. I scrutinized the date. He'd pulled out the funds the day before the shooting. Hopefully he'd had a plan.

DGH was my second stop, and I asked the desk clerk to locate Vic Dumont. She frowned at her lists, spoke through the phone, and asked me to sit and wait. I stalked around the waiting room, too anxious to sit still. Surely Vic was okay—why else would he need money? But when the nurse arrived and asked me to join her in a private room, my heart sank.

"I'm sorry to tell you this," she said, "but Mr. Dumont arrived here DOA."

My breathing stopped and my heart froze in my chest, as surely as if Angel had shocked me. Eventually I whispered, "Cause of death?"

"Gunshot wounds."

I pulled myself upright and hurried out the door. Did he die because I left? Could I have saved him? I thought about visiting his body in the morgue but knew I couldn't bear the sight.

Coward! That word echoed in my brain until I longed to shoot myself and lie down right beside him. I'd lost my whole squad, now Ron and Vic, and Laura had squelched the future I'd been planning. Why had I even cared about her? About friends? It wasn't as if I had a future.

Shaking my head free of gloomy thoughts, I recalled Vic's deepening depression, his struggle with narcotics and confession to the cops. Had he planned and committed suicide?

Driving down Woodward, I turned one street past our house and parked in front of Marcos' home. When I knocked, his mother—a handsome black woman with intelligent dark eyes—opened the door.

"I'm Pete Martin from the street behind you? Marcos did little jobs for me." I looked up as Marcos ran across the room. He hugged me and unexpected tears sprang to my eyes.

"They shoot your friend?" he asked, staring up at my face. I nodded, too choked to say a word.

"Sit down." His mother gestured toward a chair. As I sat, she went into the kitchen and brought us each a cup of tea. Sitting across from me, she said, "Marcos told me all about his job. It made him very proud to earn real money."

The tea and her calm voice helped. "I feared for him with all the shootin'—wanted to make certain he was safe."

His mother's face crinkled, caught between fear and a small smile. "Thank you for carin' about him."

Marcos grabbed my hand. "You leaving?"

"Afraid so, little man. But before I go, you gotta promise somethin'."

His eyes filled with tears, which tore my heart, and I breathed deeply to steady my own voice. "Promise me you'll stay safe. I plan to come back here in ten years and see you grown—a happy, healthy, educated man. Do you promise to stay safe, not do anythin' real stupid?"

He sniffed and nodded.

I hugged him, sticking a five into his hand.

"Bye, Marcos."

"Bye, Pete." He raised his fist. I tapped it with mine, and we slapped hands.

From their house, I cut through the back yard to our street. The old house looked peaceful, the trees just leafing out, the sky a hazy blue with fluffy clouds drifting slowly. Detroit would be a lovely city if the people could stop killing one another.

The police had stretched yellow tape across our porch, but I stepped around it and tested the front door. It was unlocked. Opening it slowly, I walked into a deafening silence.

Stepping into the parlor, I froze, staring at bloodstains on the rug. Disgust and rage overwhelmed me. Déjà vu confused images of Ron and Cole, of Vic and Rog'. Had Lee been right all along? Had I spent the last year reliving my past horror, reenacting that night in Vietnam? While I was remembering, had I endangered friends?

Running from the surging tide of emotions, I drove straight to Royal Oak and pounded hard on Dr. Freedman's door. His wife answered, staring up at me wide-eyed. "Does he expect you?"

"I'm sorry, but there's been a…an accident. Is Dr. Freedman here?"

As I spoke, he stepped into the foyer behind her. "Pete? Why are you here?"

"May I talk with you, please?"

He frowned but motioned me inside. "What's wrong?"

His wife disappeared upstairs, so I answered bluntly. "There was a shooting at my house. Vic died."

Dr. Freedman motioned me toward his office. Reaching the door, I was relieved to find neatly filed bookshelves, his pipe in a clean ashtray, and our familiar chairs. I sat down with a deep sigh.

"Were you involved?" he asked.

I shook my head. "Vic warned me ahead of time, ordered me to run. I did, but for some reason he stayed. I don't understand, unless he'd planned a suicide."

"Do you know why they shot him?"

"I guess he knew too much."

"You were fond of him?"

"He was my friend." I choked on the word, thinking of all the friends I'd lost.

Regaining control, I cut to the real question. "My childhood buddy, Lee, said comin' to Detroit was my way of reenactin' the trauma from 'Nam. You think that's what I did? Set myself up, set my friends up, so they would die?"

Dr. Freedman leaned back, prepared and lit his pipe, and puffed in silence for a time. "What do you think?"

"In some ways, yes. I confused friends here with friends in 'Nam. I chose to stay and work where it was dangerous and violent, and I took unnecessary risks. But in part that's just the way I am. I don't know how much is me, how much is just plain *crazy*." I held my face between my hands.

"Does it matter?"

I frowned. "People died, and I'm not sure what part I played."

Dr. Freedman put down his pipe. "So many factors in our lives interact simultaneously at any given moment that it's impossible to pinpoint all the blame. Your presence, your actions may have played a part, but if you didn't pull the trigger, or intentionally lead that person to his death, most people would call you innocent. Do you feel guilty?"

I nodded.

"Do you feel guilty about your friends in 'Nam?"

"I would have died to save them!" I knew that wish was fantasy, but why did this keep happening? "I hate violence, hate guns, hate death, but I'm always drawn toward them. Am I nuts?"

Dr. Freedman sighed. "I could wish to go back and rescue people—mothers, fathers, and children—murdered in the camps. But I cannot, nor can you. We are human, Pete. Being a mere human limits us, and that makes us all a little crazy." His gentle smile reminded me of Jake. "Stick with helping others, and you will do fine. Let God bear the burden for creating humans."

"But I miss them." A tsunami of grief washed over me, and tears poured down my face.

Dr. Freedman waited until I became calm. He handed me some tissues, saying, "Those you love are never far away."

His words reconnected me with Jake, and that familiar presence soothed me. "Thanks, Dr. Freedman. Thanks for seein' me again. I probably won't be back, but I wanted you to know these sessions helped."

The doctor smiled, but when I stood and turned to leave, his face wrinkled with concern. "This is yours." He handed me my sketchpad, which I'd forgotten at the end of my last session. "Take good care of yourself, Pete."

"Thanks." I grabbed my drawings. "I'll try."

Chapter 18

Night found me in a motel on the outskirts of Toledo. I'd done all I could, even found a glass shop to repair my car's rear window, but I still couldn't sleep. My work with Dr. Freedman had barely begun when my life in Detroit blew apart, exploding my mind into so many painful pieces, I was reeling. Vic died, Laura left me, and our communal home was now a crime scene. I could never again live in Detroit. Hurting like a beat dog, tail between my legs, I knew that God was punishing me.

The next morning I began the long trip home, still struggling with strong feelings about Laura and Vic. I cared less about the money, although I found its disappearance puzzling. By evening I had reached Cedar Bluff where I stopped for a bite and the chance to call Lee.

"Pete! Where are you?"

"Knoxville. You got a piece of floor and a blanket for the night?"

"You've left Detroit?"

"Yeah. In a hail of bullets."

"Shit!"

I heard real distress in his voice and wondered if I'd caught him studying for exams. "You busy?"

"No. Actually you're just in time for my graduation."

"Cool! You still plannin' on law school?"

"In the fall. Come on over and we'll talk."

Lee met me at the door to his apartment, beers in hand. We settled in as I told him the long saga about Vic, the communal house, the riots, and an edited version of my part in the drug war. I left out shooting the enforcer, my arrest for murder, and the torture. But even so, Lee's eyes grew wide before they slowly narrowed in disgust.

"You were right," I concluded. "I relived my shit from 'Nam. But somehow relivin' it allowed me to remember. I even talked a few times with a shrink." Finally I told him everything I could about my last mission overseas.

Before I'd finished, Lee looked sick. Squinting fiercely, his gaze burned a hole into my face. "Are you done playing Superman, old friend? 'Cause you have no right to be alive. Don't keep going back, reworking the same old shit, until you end up dead or in the clink."

The anger behind his words surprised me. "I can't go back, not to Detroit or Vietnam."

"Are you ready to try school?"

I shrugged. "I need to see my folks first—then decide."

Lee shook his head slowly. "Rick's stuck in prison, are you headed there as well?"

"No." That explained part of Lee's reaction. Good thing I didn't share how close I came.

Lee nodded, but worry lingered in his eyes. "If you get in too deep, I can't help, not even with a law degree, not even as a judge. You understand?"

I pursed my lips. Lee had a habit of reading between lines, and he knew I'd been in serious trouble.

"Did Ricky ask for help?"

Lee shook his head. "I wish he had. He didn't get a fair shake."

"I'm real sorry."

"We grew up together—the three Musketeers. With both of you gone, I've felt like the lone survivor. Not that Knoxville is at all like Vietnam, but I'm really, really glad to have you here."

* * *

The next day, I drove home to Walnut Springs. Ma met me at the door, her blue eyes wide. "Pete!" She grabbed me tight. "You never called. Lee had to tell us you were in Detroit."

"Sorry."

Entering the house was like a slap in the face. It took me back to my fight with Pa. Suddenly my nose ached, but the rage and shame hurt even worse. I turned away from Ma and ran upstairs to my room. Tossing my bag down, I glared out the window, focusing hard on our path into the woods. I'd been gone another year, but in this house, this room, nothing changed.

Someone coughed. Puzzled, I crossed the hall into my parents' bedroom.

"Pa?" I stared in shock. Pa never slept through the day. "Are you sick?"

"Heart attack." He pulled his skinny body up to sitting.

I stared in shock at his pallor, the weakness in his grip, and the loss of muscle in his arms. "When did it happen?"

"Right after you left. They kept me in the hospital a month, but since then I been home. Cain't even work."

"You have any money comin' in?"

"Disability from work." He shrugged. "Keep thinkin' I'll get better and go back."

"What does the doctor say?"

Pa stared at the wall. "He keeps tellin' me to go and see this heart specialist, but that takes too much money. My heart either heals up or it don't."

My own heart constricted, wondering if I'd caused him any damage with my punch. This changed everything—I would not let them go hungry. "We'll talk more," I said, standing up.

Ma fixed me a snack as I sat down at the table, eyes glued to my plate. Finally I looked up. "Lee gave you my address. You could've written, told me."

"We're okay."

"How long before the disability runs out?"

"Another month."

"And then?"

She shrugged. "God will provide."

I stalked out the door and started up my car, needing a private word with God. Was this yet another punishment? Was I doomed to rot here, caretaker to my folks? Surely God had something better planned. But then He'd provided opportunities enough—I had failed.

Stuffing my emotions, I drove into Oak Ridge and turned left onto the turnpike. At the Methodist Hospital, I asked if they had jobs. The clerk referred me to a desk at the back. I waited there. The lady who joined me asked about my training.

"I was a Navy corpsman."

"Honorable discharge?"

I looked down.

"Any further schooling? Certificates, degrees?"

Shaking my head, I raised pleading eyes.

The lady smiled sweetly. "I'm afraid we don't have a position at this time, but if you upgrade your résumé, check back."

I left in silence, angry with myself. In Cedar Bluff, I stopped at the first construction site. The Super asked me what I did.

"Framin', roofin', drywall."

"All we're needin' now are masons. You might try UT. I think they're buildin' a library down there."

I drove to UT and stopped at the deli, spotting Bruce, the Navy guy who'd talked with me last year. He waved and joined me.

"How's life treating you?" he asked.

I shook my head. "Just got back from Detroit. Been workin' there. But Pa had a heart attack, so now I need a job."

"You were a corpsman, right?"

"Yeah, but that doesn't cut it at civilian hospitals. I need a degree or certificate or somethin'. I was told I could find construction work nearby."

Bruce rolled his eyes. "You won't find good paying jobs near campus." His forehead furrowed as he ate. "What about

Eastern State, the psychiatric hospital? Would you be okay with working there?"

"Doin' what?"

"Psych tech." He checked my face. "I worked there one summer. They take the serious crazies and need men to control 'em, although if you're good you can mostly talk 'em down. Once the men get on meds, they're pretty mellow. But it's kind of depressing, seeing what happens to those folks out on the street. When they're crazy, they can't protect themselves."

I frowned, wondering if I'd like that kind of job. "How much does it pay?"

"That's the good news." He smiled. "Three bucks an hour, more with experience."

My eyebrows peaked. "Thanks. I'll check it out."

I found Eastern State out on Northshore Drive—a group of brick buildings near Fort Loudon Lake, surrounded by a high metal fence. The grounds were mostly grass, a few big trees, and well maintained. I stopped at a building marked Admissions and walked in.

"Can I help you?" The old lady at the desk looked up.

"I came to ask about a job."

"You need the office." She pointed out the window to a larger brick building down the street.

"Thanks." I walked outside, watching as a group of older women strolled past, followed by an attractive nurse. They didn't look that crazy, mostly sad. Reaching the office building, I asked the cute desk clerk if they had any jobs.

"What's your training?"

"Navy corpsman. I was lookin' to work as a psych tech."

She pulled out two sheets and handed them to me. "Fill out this application, and I'll need to see a copy of your discharge."

I sat down and read through the application, most of which was standard. I wrote down my training, my duties on the ship, and my job description out with the Marines. I decided to include my volunteer work at the clinic but skipped my brief time at DGH. The remaining slots I filled in with construction work. It was not the total truth, but I wanted my recovery time from flashbacks and torture off the record.

The resulting application didn't read all that bad. I handed her the form along with my general discharge, fearing that would damn me beyond help. I waited, watching the sun drift toward the west, remembering sunsets from our porch, from Jake's shed. Thinking about sunsets, I relaxed.

"Sorry to take so long. The nurse would like to see you."

Straightening up, I discovered the desk clerk standing by me and realized I must have nodded off. Surprised I could relax here, I rose and followed her into a private office. Behind the desk, an older, stern-faced lady motioned for me to take a chair. Without ever smiling, she eyed me up and down.

"Any physical injuries or other limitations?"

"No, ma'am."

"Any psychiatric diagnoses?"

I bit my lip and chose to tell a partial truth. "I spent two years in Vietnam, the second year out with the Marines. On my last mission, the V-C killed everyone in my squad but me. What

I saw that night still gives me trouble, and when I worked in the ER, some injuries upset me. But I don't expect to have that problem here."

She studied my face, reread my application, and handed my discharge back to me. "We have a position on the men's acute unit, but first you'll need to take a class. It teaches you techniques for handling violent patients—safe methods for containment and control. What you learned in the Marine Corps is not to be used here. Our two-week training program begins next week on Monday, eight a.m. If you complete that program with good marks, you have a job."

I felt a huge weight lift off my chest. "Pay?"

"Two dollars an hour for the training. Three if you pass and get the job." She smiled at my grin. "I'll see you Monday."

I drove home, arriving just in time for supper. Pa had made it downstairs to the table. "I found a job, but it's in Knoxville— Eastern State."

Pa's face drew into a deep frown. "You plan to work with crazies?"

"Yeah. It pays three bucks an hour once I'm trained."

His frown disappeared.

"That's a long commute," Ma said.

"I'll stay with Lee."

Ma sighed, relief softening her face.

After supper, while Pa napped on the sofa, I remained in the kitchen to help Ma. "I'm gonna send you half my check, but don't tell Pa. Promise?"

"You don't have to do that."

"If I can't, I won't. But sharin' with Lee should help me out."

That evening I called Lee, and he welcomed the news. "We'll get a one bedroom, put twin beds in the bedroom, and keep the living room for guests."

I preferred a bedroom of my own, but prices near UT were higher than Detroit. This could work. Reclaiming my rucksack, I spent the weekend on his floor.

Chapter 19

The training at Eastern State proved easy, and my new job was similar to an LPN's—on steroids. I helped patients with anything they couldn't, or wouldn't, do themselves. Getting patients through admissions proved the hardest step. The new admits had to shower, be deloused, and dress in our uniform of puke-green pajamas. The doctors wouldn't see them until then.

Strangely enough, my experience with flashbacks seemed to help. I understood the patients' paranoia, their over-reactions to taking off their clothes, getting wet, and being doused with turpentine. I took extra time to explain things, give them choices. Most folks responded if you didn't push too hard. The craziest folks were the ones high on drugs. If I couldn't reason with them, I left them in seclusion 'til they cleared.

Once past the entry point, most clients improved, responding to the care, food, and safety on the unit with varying levels of relief. After that pills became the psych tech's battleground. We gave antipsychotics to our hallucinating crowd. The suicidal patients usually received tricyclics. A few patients would refuse, requiring court orders, and others suffered serious side effects.

We added anticholinergic meds to stop muscle twitches, Milk of Magnesia for constipation, and lots of water for dry mouths.

Some people did well on medication, transforming quickly into "normal" human beings with all the quirks that word implies. Others showed little or no change. And some switched from mania into deep depression, silenced and blinded to the world.

I kept an eye out for other veterans, learning quickly that the staff—even the psychiatrists—had trouble identifying flashbacks. Post Traumatic Stress Disorder was the latest label for a problem as old as all mankind. But since I'd grown up with Pa, lived with Jake, and suffered through too many flashbacks of my own, I recognized the symptoms instantly.

The first veteran I met, a young black man, tried to punch me out when I approached him with his shot. The other techs held him while I gave the injection. Afterwards I made an effort to be friends. His name was Buck, short for Buckley, and he'd lived in Alabama until he enlisted in the Army. After a few days, he knew my name, and we talked about his missions on three different deployments into 'Nam. He didn't like people in his face, my first mistake, and he was terrified of needles.

"Why aren't you at the VA?" I asked.

He scowled. "After what they put me through, I should trust 'em?"

I reported his preferences to the treatment team, and the doctor changed his meds from shots to pills. Our battles ended. But Buck still complained about things messing with his head, giving him nightmares and weird visions. When he told me the dreams and visions were from 'Nam, we kept talking.

I had neither Jake's experience nor Dr. Freedman's expertise, but I tried my best to listen, to interpret the "dilemmas" his traumatic memories posed—especially the ones he hid away. Little by little, Buck began to think more clearly, accept what happened, and have fewer "crazy" intrusions in his life. A month later he left, still on meds but smiling, and he thanked me. The treatment team assigned me to another veteran.

* * *

Lee and I did okay in our one-bedroom apartment, except he kept our table covered up in books, which meant clearing it every time we ate. I annoyed him by running up the phone bill and chatting with Laura late into the night. But thanks to Lee's logic and good sense, we stayed friends.

Our conversations ranged from girls to politics, especially the upcoming presidential election and the death of Robert Kennedy. That assassination made Nixon a shoo-in—not that I really cared. Laura weighed in with a vote for Hubert Humphrey, while Lee's vote would be Republican.

One day I visited the UT Hospital and asked about classes to become a paramedic. They had a six-week refresher course for corpsman, so I switched to the evening shift at work. By the end of the class, I'd earned my license and signed on with the UT ambulance crew.

Proud of this success, I called Laura. I hadn't said a word before, fearing I might fail. As we chatted, I bragged about my EMT license and getting a better paying job.

She didn't sound impressed. "You left your job at Eastern State?"

"Yeah. I'm workin' on an ambulance now. It pays more and gives me more chances to save lives."

"Pete." Laura sighed, a sound that meant frustration—usually with me. "Remember what happened at the ER and the clinic? You sure you want to do this—be the first responder at accidents and murders—after everything you've already seen?"

My hackles rose. "That's exactly what I've trained for."

"But is this a job you'll enjoy?"

"It's no different than you working as a nurse," I snapped.

She sighed again. "Okay. Try it for a week, and then call back."

My first week was easy. We saved a heart-attack victim, an old man suffering a stroke, and a child with a broken leg. I thought I'd found my calling. The next weekend, I phoned Laura.

"I love it. I'm good at it. This is right where I belong."

"Great! I'm delighted you enjoy your job." She sounded relieved, and I realized she'd been worrying about me.

"How's your work?"

"Super. I'm on the pediatric floor. Adore the kids!"

I smiled, daring to dream about a future where Laura and I married and had kids.

The next week went much like the first. In fact it was nearly spring before I faced a problem. A lethal combination of icy roads, a stoned trucker with an overloaded semi, and a family with children headed south for spring break led to a frantic 911 call.

Our team arrived first, weaving through stopped traffic until we found the semi jack-knifed on its back. The car had slid beneath the truck, hitting with such force that the impact sliced the roof off. Pieces of the family lay strewn on the road.

I took one look at the scene and found myself in 'Nam, surrounded by a squadron of V-C. I started running. Slipping and falling on the ice brought me around. My buddy helped me back into the cab, and he spent the next two hours filling bags with body parts. When the road was clear of all human remains, he rejoined me in the truck.

"It's okay, Pete. We all have our moments. I won't tell."

I don't recall thanking him or even driving home. Lee asked me what happened, and when I couldn't tell him, he called and spoke with Laura before handing me the phone.

"Laura?" I croaked.

"Hey, Pete. Lee said you're acting strange. Are you in a flashback?"

I wanted to scream, to tell both Lee and Laura to leave me the hell alone, but somewhere deep inside, I knew the truth. Struggling to find words, I said, "We were first responders to a battle…"

"What happened in this battle?"

"They all died!" I yelled, and suddenly it hit me. That's what happened back in 'Nam.

She paused. "Are you sure this is what you want to do?"

"Fuck!" I screamed into the phone. "It's not what I want! They're all dead! There's nothin' I can do. I hate that. You know how much I hate that!"

Laura remained silent for a minute. "If you hate it so much, why take a job that puts you on the front lines—again? I love you, Pete. But you really need to give yourself a break."

I slammed the phone into its cradle. Lee watched as I stormed outside, heading for my car until I realized I didn't have my keys. Damn Lee! I came back inside and sat down, head in hands. Lee pulled up a chair.

"I can't go on like this!" I shrieked. "Can't do what I like, can't be with Laura, wasted money on classes and can't even do the work. I'm such a failure!" Grabbing my sketchpad, I started tearing up the pictures.

Lee snatched it from my hands. "Don't destroy those, Pete. That's a history of your life." He smoothed out a sketch I made in 'Nam. "Who are they?"

I stared at Rog', Cole, and Newt sitting by our barracks. Guilt and grief at their deaths pulled me down, drowning me. Seeing no other option, I picked up my .45, inserted the clip, and chambered the first round.

"Whoa, Pete. Give me that." Lee reached out his hand. "You don't wanna do this—not to Laura or me."

I held the muzzle firmly to my head. Clicking off the safety and taking a deep breath, I closed my eyes.

Lee grabbed the barrel, pulling it away, and I fought back.

"Don't shoot *me*!" Lee screamed.

His panicked voice popped my eyes wide open, revealing my .45 pointed straight at him. Horrified, I dropped the pistol's grip into his hand. He put the safety on and ran outside. I froze—staring.

Shortly he returned without the gun. I remained staring and unmoving as he brought a glass of water and a pill.

"Here, take this. You need to sleep."

"Lee." I met his eyes and barely shook my head. "I would never…"

"I know, but you just scared me shitless. Please take the pill and go to sleep."

The terror in his eyes had dissipated, and now they crinkled with concern. I took the pill and swallowed. But as I fully comprehended what I'd almost done, I prayed to die.

"We're gonna be okay," Lee said, reading my fears. "No harm. No foul."

Before long, I stretched out on the couch. But after about an hour's rest, I woke—screaming. Lee came from the bedroom, eyes half-open.

"You had another nightmare. Why don't you go to bed?"

I stumbled into the bedroom and curled up on my mattress, too wired to sleep, my mind rehashing 'Nam. Running from the V-C, a swarm of bullets whistled past and sliced into the jungle growth ahead. I should have died.

Lee sat hunched on his bed across the room, staring at me through drooping lids. After a while, he brought another pill. When that kicked in, I finally slept.

Lee woke me the next morning. "Are you going back to work?"

I shook my head. There was no point in a job I couldn't do. That fact made me sick. I made me sick. The whole fucking world made me sick!

"Find another job. You still owe rent." Lee slammed the door on his way out.

Easy for him to say, but when you've failed at everything you love, where do you start? I recalled my last job in Detroit—stacking bricks. That's all I was good for—just like Pa. But Laura wouldn't marry an uneducated loser. Had I really hung up on her? Threatened to shoot Lee? Anxiety grabbed me by the balls. What if Lee threw me out and Laura wouldn't listen?

I jumped up, but Lee had my .45 and car keys. Hands shaking, I searched the fridge, finding and eating all the leftover pizza. That calmed me enough to make a short-term plan. Showered and dressed, I hiked to the Ag campus and found an inviting grassy spot.

I sat gazing into space until a veterinary student brought an old horse out to graze. I watched as the animal munched happily on grass, and its slow, graceful movements soothed my soul.

I was starting to relax when a familiar face appeared.

"Pete? What you doing here?" Bruce asked, settling uninvited on the grass nearby.

I looked down, and he examined me with sympathetic eyes. "Life been messing with you lately?"

I shrugged.

We both focused on a new horse coming out. The young stallion reared, trumpeted and pawed, announcing his presence loudly to the world. His coat gleamed gold, rippling over muscle.

"Now that is a horse." Bruce smiled. "Gotta love his spirit." When I didn't respond, he eyed me thoughtfully. "You ever see the UT gardens?"

I shook my head.

He rose, nodding toward a green field behind us. "Follow me. I think you're gonna like this."

Somewhat reluctantly, I followed. He led the way among traditional flowerbeds, their roses and peonies just starting to leaf out, and turned along a well-worn path. The trail led us beneath a row of flowering cherries, our steps softened by the petals underfoot. Next we passed budding dogwoods and newly opened redbuds.

"They have all my favorite trees, but today you gotta see the wildflowers." Bruce took a side path toward the woods.

I moved up beside him to better read his face. "I thought you were studyin' to be an engineer?"

"I am." He looked down. "But I'm a farmer at heart, and some days I need a dose of home."

"Where's home?"

"Middlesboro. My family has a big spread, even horses."

I glanced quickly at his injured hand, realizing Bruce would never be a farmer—same as I would never be an EMT.

Bruce noted the direction of my gaze. "'Nam changed my plans."

"Yeah—afraid it changed mine too."

He slowed and turned, one eyebrow raised in question.

He'd advised against talking years ago, but now he seemed to have a change of heart. "I keep tryin' to do what I once loved, but in tight situations where I used to keep my cool, now I panic." I grabbed my head.

He sighed and nodded slowly. "Can you see yourself doing something else?"

I thought about the job he helped me find. "I worked all last year at Eastern State, but I never saw that job as a career."

"Unless you study social work or go to med school."

My mind jumped to Dr. Freedman. He'd survived a living hell, and now he used his experience to help others—just like Jake did years ago. Could I, with training, do the same?

When we reached the wildflowers, Bruce slowed to a stop. The bare oaks and walnut trees towering overhead reminded me of those down by our creek. Almost hidden in the dead leaves on the forest floor, white and yellow trillium opened fragile blossoms. A sea of tiny iris, intermixed with dainty snowdrops, surrounded the clumps of trillium. And at the edge of the forest, daffodils grew, nodding their golden heads towards the morning sun.

A smile slowly crept across my face.

Bruce grinned. "Gotta go. I have a big exam today and just needed a walk to calm my nerves. See you around."

"Good luck—and thanks."

I hurried back to our apartment and called Eastern State, asking if they had any openings for a psych tech. The nurse recognized my name and pulled my file. When I told her I was now a licensed EMT, she offered a position with more pay.

Next I called the UT ambulance service and told them I took another job. They wished me luck. I waited to phone Laura, calling as soon as she got home.

"Laura, honey, I'm so sorry! I didn't mean to hang up like I did."

"Pete! You sound better. Can you tell me what happened?"

"A car—cut in two—body parts scattered all over the highway. I got so confused, I couldn't work." Saying it aloud made me feel stupid.

"I'm thrilled you're okay! Working as an EMT is dangerous for you, and there are so many other ways you can help people. Please stop being stubborn and choose a different path."

For once I was ahead of her advice. "I'm goin' back to work at Eastern State—with a raise."

"That's wonderful!" I heard the smile in her voice. "Love you, Pete."

* * *

When Lee came home that evening, he caught me filling out a UT application. I looked up. "My credits mostly transfer, so I didn't completely waste my time."

Lee collapsed on the sofa, eyes bagged with fatigue. "What you planning to major in?"

"Pre-med."

He glared at me. "Shit, Pete! Don't you know enough to quit?"

I met his angry stare with confusion. "I thought you wanted me in school."

"I do. But I can't stay up nights, keeping you alive every time you see a body part. Are you sure this is something you can do?"

I began to argue, but then I recalled my suicide attempt and how he took my .45 away. "I'm so sorry…"

Lee shrugged. "I'm okay about last night, but I don't want to make a habit of it."

I nodded, aware of his exhaustion. "I'm not too sure about the school part, but Eastern State just gave me a big raise. You think I'd make a good psychiatrist?"

His eyes widened. "It's cool you got more money. But eight years of school, Pete? Are you serious?"

"Yeah." I scrutinized his face.

Lee's expression relaxed into a thoughtful smile. "If you can make it through, you'll be great."

Chapter 20

I started UT in the fall of '69, and the next two years flew past in a blur. I ran from classes to work, squeezing studies in between, interspersed with Laura's phone calls and visits with my folks. I fought money problems, school problems, exhaustion, disappointment, and periods of total self-disgust. But with everybody's help, I kept picking up the pieces and moving slowly toward my goal.

Like the year I spent on the Sanctuary ship, time ran by so quickly that only the highest and lowest points stood out. Sarah and Bailey tied the knot. Lee found a girlfriend—a beautiful, intelligent, Latina named Maria—and we three moved into a two-bedroom apartment. Shortly thereafter Ma threatened to leave Pa. That was in June of 1970.

Ma called me, her voice angry. "He lies in bed all day, won't take his medicine, won't go outside. It's like he's waiting there to die, and I can't watch it!"

"You want me to talk with him?" I doubted that would work.

"If you can talk—not start a fight. He doesn't hear anything I say."

My mind puzzled over Pa's resistance, but my work at Eastern State helped me face it logically. Feeling powerless and sick might be triggering past trauma, like the horrible year he spent in a POW camp. If that were the case, I'd need to tread lightly, but I had an idea that might work.

"Okay, on Sunday."

Ma met me on the porch when I arrived. "He's given up. But I still love him, and I can't let him go. I just can't!" She started crying. I hugged her, but she pulled away, shaking her head. "Don't waste your time with me. Talk to him."

Surprised by the anger in her voice, I stepped back, recalling her behavior when I was only ten and she'd projected her guilt and rage on me. Climbing the stairs, I found Pa still in bed. He didn't even turn when I walked in.

"Hey, Pa." I walked around, pulling up a chair where he could see. "Ma's upset. Do you know what's buggin' her?"

"Yeah," he grunted. "I cain't work."

I shook my head. "I think she's more scared of losin' you."

He stayed silent for some time.

Finally I asked. "You gettin' worse?"

He shrugged and pulled himself to sitting, coughing from that minimal exertion. "I ain't worth wastin' a bullet in my head."

I knew the feeling all too well. "That's not what she's thinkin', Pa. She loves you so much, she thinks her life will be over when you die."

He turned away. I knew how much he loved her—worshipped her.

"Could you do her one more favor?"

"What?"

"See the specialist your doctor recommended?"

"It'd be a waste of time and money." Pa leaned back against the headboard and fixed me with his stare, a look that used to turn my blood to ice.

I faced him without flinching. "Maybe for you, but not for her."

He dropped his eyes, and I held my breath. After a minute he looked up. "Would you take me?"

My mind jumped to my schedule, wondering how I'd manage, but I nodded. "Sure."

"Okay."

I got the details from Ma, called for an appointment, and rearranged my schedule to include a half-day off. Pa was up and dressed before I arrived, sitting in the living room in his favorite chair. When I offered to help him to the car, he stood and walked, painfully slow, but on his own.

The cardiologist worked at Methodist in Oak Ridge. Pa still refused to visit the VA, based on a bad experience years ago. But this doctor had served in WWII, and I hoped that would help Pa to connect.

We had to wait, and Pa fidgeted the whole time, griping about doctors—especially heart specialists—who were such know-it-alls they couldn't even see you on time. I bit my tongue, treating him like any other patient, although I ached to say *shut up*.

Finally Dr. White called us back. He already had a copy of Pa's chart, but he took time listening to Pa's version of his history before he listened to his heart. Then he ordered an EKG, an X-ray, and an ultrasound—a new test that worked, best I understood, like sonar. As we waited for results, I realized Pa had settled down.

"So what do you think of him?" I asked.

"He's okay."

From Pa that was high praise indeed.

Once the tests were complete, we met back with the doctor. By now Pa was paying close attention. Dr. White pulled up a chair. "You're a strong man, Mr. Martin. You suffered a serious heart attack, which has left a big scar across your heart. That means it can't beat as strongly as it once did—but it's beating. There are a couple things you can do to help your heart beat a little stronger."

I watched Pa's face, and he was listening. When he didn't ask questions, Dr. White continued. "You're blood pressure is low, far too low for you to feel good. Have you noticed that you're dizzy, can't think as clearly as you did before?"

Pa frowned.

"That also makes your legs swell and keeps fluid in your lungs. Do you have trouble breathing when you sleep?"

Pa nodded.

"I'm ordering an old fashioned medicine for you, one that's been used for over a century. But it works."

I glanced at the prescription he handed Pa—digoxin.

"You need to walk. Using your legs pumps more blood into your heart, which keeps fluid off your legs and lungs and sends blood to your brain. Do you have a place where you can walk?"

"Yeah. We got a path down to the creek, good fishin' hole."

Dr. White grinned. "I love to fish."

Pa shrugged. "You're welcome anytime. Not sure I can walk that far right now."

"Once you're on the pills, you can build up your endurance. Just don't go too far too soon, and always remember you have to walk back home." The doctor raised an eyebrow.

"How long will it take?"

"The medicine will take about a week, but it may take months to build endurance. And since your heart is scarred, it will never be as strong as it once was. Are you on disability?"

"Ran out."

"You should talk to the VA. From what your records show, your country owes you a huge debt. It's time we paid." He looked my father in the eye with genuine respect. Always the Marine, Pa straightened his spine and nodded back.

On the trip home, I stopped and bought his pills, handing him the bottle as I climbed into the car. "You gonna take 'em?"

"Yep."

At home I coaxed Ma to apply to the VA, and after all the paperwork was done, Pa received a small but livable paycheck. From then on, Ma refused any portion of my pay. But the real reward came when Dr. White paid us a visit, and Pa walked down to the creek with him to fish. I sat on the porch and sketched two proud, aging veterans marching off with their fishing poles and smiles. Ma's grin almost split her face.

Chapter 21

The next year at school, I felt more confident, mastering both my work and the most challenging of my science classes. That lasted until September 1971 when Laura's call abruptly changed our lives. Shortly after midnight, I arrived home from work—ready for a good night's sleep before my day at school—when I saw the answering machine blinking. The voice was Laura's, but she was crying so hard I couldn't make out what she said. Ignoring the late hour, I called back.

Laura picked up immediately. "Pete, thank God! You might understand, but I can't, I just can't. It doesn't make any sense!"

"What happened?"

"Mom and Dad! I never thought he'd do this. Never! I should've done something—committed him, or at the very least gotten him a doctor. I never dreamed he'd actually do it!"

"What'd he do?" My imagination ran away with me, and I hoped what I feared wasn't true.

"He shot them both!" Laura sobbed.

I wished I could take her in my arms. Waiting until she calmed down enough to listen, I asked, "Are you okay?"

"I was at work. I didn't realize today was any different. I

still don't know if it was an anniversary, or if something just set him off. I came home and found them on the floor—in the kitchen with his shotgun—all that blood!"

I closed my eyes, picturing the scene. "Where are you now?"

"Upstairs in my room. I called the police, and they came and took the bodies, but I can't bring myself to clean it up. I really can't."

"Then don't. I'll come help. If I leave now, I should be there by early afternoon. Have you eaten?"

"No. The kitchen…"

"Is there any place nearby that stays open?"

"I think—maybe Kroger's?"

"Is there a motel near the Kroger's?"

"Yes."

"You go to Kroger's and buy yourself some food. Then go to the motel and try to sleep. I'm on my way—be there by tomorrow. Can you do that?"

"Yes, but what about the cows?"

I didn't know whether to groan or laugh, but she was right— I'd forgotten all about their livestock. "You could go back in the mornin' and milk cows. Or even go to work—if that feels safe. I'm comin' as quickly as I can."

When I finally hung up, Lee stuck his head into the hall. "What's up?"

"Laura's pa lost it; killed himself and her ma. I'm headin' north."

"Whoa!" Lee stared at me, his expression worried. "Will you be okay?"

189

"Yeah. The police already came and got the bodies."

Lee nodded. "Good. Drive safe. Want me to call your job?"

"Yeah, thanks."

I stuffed clothes and toiletries into my rucksack and took off. It didn't seem that far to Cincinnati, but the trip across Ohio went on and on. Somewhere near the border, I almost fell asleep, but I made it to the nearest rest stop. Locking my car, I curled up for a nap.

I woke to an angry man pounding on my windshield. Scared and confused, I pulled my gun. He eyed the .45 and quickly backed away.

I rolled down the window, pistol steady in my hand. "What you want?"

He pulled out a badge. "Are you Pete Martin?"

"Yes sir."

"I work for the State Highway Patrol. May I see your license?"

Noting the patrol car behind him, I obeyed.

"You're wanted for questioning about a double homicide somewhere up in rural Michigan."

"That's where I'm headed. My girlfriend called, said her father killed her mother and himself. I'm tryin' to get there. Just had to take a nap."

"You'll have to talk to the detective. Maybe he'll let you call your girl."

I locked up my car and handed him my pistol. He motioned me into the back seat. At least I wasn't in Detroit, but I still felt sweat prickling my skin, my heart skipping in my chest. At the station, they locked me inside an empty cell. I paced the floor until shortly after eight when a man dressed in a dark suit and tie joined me. Leaving the door ajar, he sat down on the bench, serious brown eyes meeting my gaze.

"I'm Bill Smith, detective with the FBI. You ever know a man named Vic Dumont?"

His title and question caught me totally off guard. "Yeah. He was a friend of mine a couple years back when I was workin' in Detroit."

"Know where he is?"

I flinched at his feigned ignorance. "Dead. He was murdered in a shoot-out at our house."

"You know who killed him?"

"Not for sure."

"Were you there?"

"Until Vic got a call and ordered me to leave."

"Did you work for Vic?"

"No. He was a friend, a good friend." I pushed aside my grief and focused hard on the G-man. Why was he asking about Vic? Why the Feds?

"Did you know his girlfriend?"

I frowned. "Which one?"

The detective checked his notes. "Laura Davenport."

"Yeah, she just called me. She lives with her family on a farm, works as a nurse. But last night she came home and found her ma and pa both dead. She thought her pa killed them. You have a different theory?"

The detective went out and came back with a tape. He played it, and when I heard the bass voice and the tenor with his accent,

I nodded recognition. "Those men were at our house once, but I only heard them, never saw them. Do you know who they are?"

"Top of our most wanted list, that's all. Can you tell me anything about them?"

I tried hard to think. "They drove a big black limo when they came, and later Vic said they'd broken an agreement, tortured our friends, and were comin' after him."

"Shame he died." Smith's eyes probed mine. "We sure could use that information."

I looked down, biting hard on my lip, unsure what message he was trying to convey. "Who told you to question me?" I asked.

"My superiors at the FBI. They thought you might know something useful."

I thought back to Detroit, to the man who tailed me when I picked up the heroin and who later jumped me at our house. Could he be a member of that gang?

"Almost a year before the shootin', this guy grabbed me— almost had me, but I threw him down."

"You killed him?" Smith's eyes widened.

"No, he was breathin'." I tried hard to picture my assailant. "You got some paper and a pencil? I can sketch."

He led me into a private room, opened a drawer, and pulled out drawing supplies. I drew quickly, recalling the size and shape of his body and his head, but I left the face incomplete. "It's not good. Afraid that's as much as I remember."

"Skin color?" he asked, studying my sketch.

"Caucasian, tanned, dark hair shaved real close. I'm not sure about his eyes."

He shook his head. "A lot of men match that description. You see anybody else?"

My mind flashed to the old guy in Vic's ward. "Maybe." I picked up the pencil and made a better sketch: a slight, thin man with moustache and Roman nose, piercing eyes, and gray hair thinning in the front. By the time I finished, Smith was staring.

"You know him?" I asked.

"If that's a good picture, he could be the one we want. Where did you see him?"

"In the hospital ward, about a week after they beat Vic near to death. I paid close attention 'cause this guy had a gun."

"Did he see you?"

I shrugged.

"If either he or his goon saw your face, you may be on their hit list. Stay alert."

I nodded. "May I go now? I promised Laura I'd be there by afternoon, and I'm scared for her, 'specially now you've told me it's a murder."

He frowned. "Would it help if I gave the local cops a heads up?"

"Yeah, thanks!"

"Just stay where I can reach you." Smith jotted down my address and phone number, checked me out of jail, returned my pistol, and drove me down the freeway to my car. He got out and stood staring at the rear. "Bullet holes?"

"Yeah." I ran my hand across the fender. "From the same guns that killed Vic. It was close."

"I need to make an imprint. It'll only take a sec."

"There's still a bullet in my dash. You want it?"

"Definitely."

I found a small screwdriver in my trunk and pried the slug loose.

He inspected the squashed lead. "This might prove useful."

More confused than ever, I drove off. I headed straight up to the farm, avoiding Detroit, but as I sped along the highway, my mind whirled. Why would a Detroit gang go after Laura's folks? Were they after Laura? Why now, more than three years since Vic's death?

When I finally arrived, I saw a cop car parked in the road next to their drive. I stopped and showed my license. He waved me through, and Laura met me on the porch. After hugging her close, we sat together on the swing. I listened to her story before I said a word. Then I explained about the Feds.

"They think it's murder?" Her eyes grew as big as saucers. "Why? What's this got to do with Vic?"

"I think they're huntin' down the guys who killed him. The state trooper grabbed me as soon as I crossed the Michigan state line, but an FBI detective came to do the questionin'. Sounded like they're gatherin' evidence."

Laura puzzled in silence for a while. Finally she asked, "What happened to you, back in Detroit? I know you helped Vic, maybe saved his life, but you never told me why you were arrested."

I sighed, my gaze dropping to the porch floor, but she definitely had a right to know. So I told her the whole story about shooting the enforcer. "After the shootin', Vic didn't tell the cops—said he couldn't remember anythin'. So the drug lord tried to get the truth out of Ron, then Phil, and me. We each got arrested and…" I couldn't say the word.

"Tortured?"

I bit my lip and slowly nodded. "They did worse to Vic the year before."

She frowned hard. "You think that's the reason Ron OD'd?"

"Most likely. Phil was tougher—though he did give them my name."

Laura remained quiet. I could see her mind carefully fitting all the pieces. "So my parents are dead, Ron and Vic are dead, and we're both at risk—all because of something Vic did?"

I shrugged. "When Vic confessed to murderin' their enforcer, they killed him. That doesn't explain why they're after us right now."

Laura bit her lip to stop the tears. I knew she needed time—both to grieve and to make her own decisions—but I feared the cop would leave and the gunmen would return.

"We can't stay here, sweets—it's not safe. Let's go to the motel for the night."

"And after that?" She glanced warily at me.

"I can keep you safe if you'll come to Tennessee."

She sighed, still fighting back the tears. I waited, and eventually she lifted her eyes to meet mine, nodding consent. "But first we need to take care of Dad's cows and Beauty."

I breathed out in relief, impressed, as always, by her mental toughness. I followed her into the barn where she guided me through the feeding, milking, and cleanup routines.

While Laura groomed her horse, I asked. "Have you got a plan?"

She sighed deep, burying her face in Beauty's neck. After a few minutes, she looked up. "I can sell the cows. One of our neighbors has wanted them for years."

I smiled. "Good. What about the chickens and your horse?"

"Mom sold her chickens late last year, and maybe Mr. Green will be willing to keep Beauty."

I moved closer and gave Laura a big squeeze, knowing how much she had already given up. "I promise we'll get you another horse."

As I listened in on her call to Mr. Green, I could tell he felt saddened by her parents' deaths, delighted with the cows and willing to take good care of Beauty. Unfortunately, he didn't have the cash.

Laura handled that well. "If you'll come and get them, you can make payments to Brett Smith, my family's lawyer."

When we finally opened up the door into the kitchen, the smell of rancid blood brought back ugly memories. I braced myself, wanting to be strong for Laura's sake. But since it was a crime scene, I wasn't sure how to proceed.

Laura focused on the window, eyes avoiding the blood. "The cops were here all morning, told me they were done. So I guess it's okay to clean this up."

I mopped the floor while Laura scrubbed down the whole kitchen. Once that chore was complete, we checked the house, which her mother had kept immaculate. Last we turned down the heat, turned off the water, and locked up.

In town, while Laura made arrangements for the funeral, I walked across the street and spoke with the police. As expected, Smith had called them, and they were on alert. After that I drove Laura to her lawyer's office. She named him executor of her parents' estate and asked him to list the farm for sale. I gave him my address and phone number as her contact.

The next afternoon we held a small memorial service and buried her ma and pa in the family plot. I stayed jumpy, watching every car, but the local cops attended, and no black limos appeared. By nightfall, we'd packed our cars with all they could hold and headed south.

* * *

When I brought Laura home to our apartment, I feared Lee and Maria would resent her, feel crowded. Instead they welcomed her with open arms. I would have been ecstatic, except Laura stayed so sad—at least at first. Once her nursing license transferred and she landed a good job at Children's Hospital nearby, her mood improved. That's when we started to make plans. I would graduate that spring and had applied to medical schools. Wherever I went, Laura promised she'd come too.

Remembering what Smith said, I did my best to burglarproof our place. When I finally told Lee the whole ugly story, he grew frightened and then angry. But once we worked that through, he helped. We put new deadbolts on the doors, hacked phone lines into all the rooms and moved our desks near windows—so we could keep watch on the entrances below. I obtained a permit to carry my pistol and kept it on me everywhere I went. It wasn't legal at UT, but given the alternative, I chose to take the lesser risk.

Returning to work, I found the place in chaos. An unannounced inspection had discovered overcrowding and even found patients sleeping on the floor. The top brass were on the firing line, and the state appointed a new medical director, Dr. Marshall, who tightened up the rules. I prayed to keep my job and ended up with a promotion.

My first acceptance letter came from UT Memphis, which guaranteed me a place in medical school. But given my childhood trauma in that city, I preferred any other spot. I checked the mail daily for a letter from my first choice, UC San Diego. But when their envelope arrived, I could tell the enclosure was too thin. Running into the apartment, I offered it to Laura.

"Open it, please. If it's a refusal, I don't wanna see."

She rolled her eyes and tore the envelope, reading the letter but not saying a word.

"Well?"

"You didn't want to see so I'm not telling."

"It's a refusal?"

"I'm not telling." She stuck the letter in her pocket and went into the kitchen to fix lunch.

I followed. "Don't do this, Laura. Give me the damn letter."

She laughed and dangled it, forcing me to grab.

I unfolded the page, skipping through the introductions to the text: *You're invited for an interview at UCSD Medical School on December 21 at 1:00 p.m.*

Chapter 22

My eyes didn't move past that line. "They want to interview me—in San Diego?" My mind jumped to Red, and I hunted for his number, hoping against hope he hadn't moved. Reassured by his voice on the machine, I left a message.

It was late evening when he called. "Doc! You devil. Where you been?"

"Sorry I took so long to call."

"It's four long years, buddy. You been staying out of trouble?"

"Not hardly."

"Tell me where you are, what you're doing."

"I'm in Knoxville, finishin' up college, but I have an interview at the UCSD med school on December twenty-first. My girlfriend, Laura, might come too. You got room?"

"Always room for you. Where'd you meet Laura?"

"In Detroit."

"What the hell were you doing in Detroit?"

"Workin', at least until I got myself in trouble."

"That sounds like a story."

"Yeah."

Red paused and then asked, "You been okay? Any problems?"

I knew what he meant. "Off and on."

"You remember any more?"

"Some, not all. I need to talk. Not over the phone, but face to face."

"Sure thing. I learned something new. Remember Cole?"

"Of course." A pang of grief stabbed me as I pictured the bullet slicing toward his head.

"He's here."

"What? I saw him shot."

"He told me. He also told me how you saved his life. When you get here, I'll put the two of you together, let you hash out all the details."

"No shit!" I felt ten pounds lighter with that news. "Tell him I can't wait." I turned my head away, breathing hard and blinking back the tears.

Red gave me a minute before asking, "So you plan to go to medical school here?"

"Maybe, if this interview works out. Are you done with school?"

"I got my BA and started a Master's in Criminal Justice."

"You headin' to law school?"

"Naw. I'm still aiming for the FBI."

That idea floored me, remembering his knee. Maybe there were desk jobs he could do. Thinking back, I recalled how he always followed rules, did everything exactly by the book. "I can see that."

"I'm excited that you're going to med school. Call when you book your flight, and either Cole or I will meet you at the airport."

I hung up the phone, jumping to my feet. Cole was alive! I turned to Laura. "I'm not the only living person in my squad. Cole survived."

"He's in California?"

"Yeah. I should've called Red years ago." I looked down, knowing I'd avoided my old friends.

"You plan to stay with him?" She smiled wistfully.

"You want to come? It would be like a vacation."

She hugged me.

We bought our airplane tickets, told Red and waited impatiently—like children before Christmas.

* * *

We left Knoxville before dawn in a cold December rain, and the weather wasn't much better in Atlanta. Because of the time change, we arrived in San Diego before noon. Red met us at the gate. He'd grown a moustache, which made him almost look his age. We hugged. When I introduced Laura, Red raised an approving eyebrow.

"Pleased to meet you, Laura. Now I know why Doc hasn't called me in four years." Red turned to me. "Cole is coming after dinner. That should leave us time to talk. Are you okay with pizza?" He glanced at Laura with concern.

Thinking he feared her reaction to our stories, I asked her, "Could you entertain yourself after supper?"

"Don't worry, Pete. I'll be so tired, I'll just crash.

Red drove me to my interview at UCSD and promised to give Laura a tour of the campus. I could tell she felt comfortable with Red and waved them off. Inside, I checked out my appearance in a restroom, hoping I looked professional enough. I introduced myself to the receptionist, who told me to have a seat. I fidgeted while waiting for at least another hour. Wanting to stay in San Diego near my friends made the minutes crawl like snails.

Eventually a tall, dark-haired man came out to greet me. "I'm Dr. Allen," he said, shaking my hand. "I'm only the first of several people you'll meet. Do you know which specialty you'll choose?"

"Not for sure. I was a Navy corpsman in 'Nam, and after I came home, I got licensed to be an EMT. But the last three years I've worked at Eastern State, a psychiatric hospital, and now I'm pretty comfortable with that."

"Any doctors in your family?"

I laughed and shook my head. "My pa's an ex-Marine and jack-of-all-trades."

Dr. Allen smiled, but I couldn't tell what he was thinking. "Your grades in college are adequate, not great, which makes your MCAT score all the more surprising. Can you explain that difference?"

I hadn't really thought about the test. "I've worked full time while in school, and sometimes that's interfered with doin' all the homework, but I also learned things on the job. As for the test, I guess I had a good night's sleep."

"You received a general discharge. Would you like to explain what happened there?"

I frowned. "I did well as a corpsman, but on my last mission my squad was ambushed, and only two of us survived. I don't know all that happened, and I guess the Navy was equally confused. They sent me home."

"Is this event under review?"

"I'm not sure, but I'm meetin' with friends tonight to try and sort it out. Hopefully I'll learn enough to upgrade my discharge."

Next I met Dr. Adams, a black pediatrician. He asked me details about my childhood. I edited the worst parts and told him I loved children. Finally I spoke with Dr. Russell, the only woman there, and the only one who taught psychiatry.

"Dr. Allen said you work at a psychiatric hospital?"

"Yes, ma'am."

"What do you do there?"

"I'm a senior psych tech. The job's taught me a lot about different diagnoses, symptoms, management, treatment, medications and also what to say and not to say. I think I've always been good at readin' people, and that helps."

She smiled and cocked her head. "Do you have any questions to ask me?"

I smiled back, grateful for the chance. "What made you choose psychiatry?"

"Well, it wasn't the money." She laughed. "I was good at surgery, and the surgeons get all the gold and glory. But what they really do is repair a body part, often the same part several times a day. Psychiatrists change people. They change the course of people's lives. Guess I'm an idealist and thought I could help make the world a better place."

"By changing one person at a time?"

"Yeah."

"Has it worked?"

She shrugged, a crooked grin across her face. "Nothing ever goes the way you plan. But yes, I've changed lives, and those people have changed me. It takes courage to look inside the human mind, and sometimes you find your own demons staring back, but it makes for one amazing trip."

It was five p.m. by the time we finished up, and I breathed out in relief when I walked outside and saw Laura waving from Red's car. As he drove us home, Laura raved. "San Diego's beyond gorgeous, and Red insists the weather is like this year 'round. Of course, it might be hard to stay inside and study when you could be sunning at the beach." She grinned at me.

I raised an eyebrow. "I'm not accepted yet."

"How'd it go?" Red asked, glancing over at my face.

"Not a clue."

We picked up a pizza and returned to his apartment. I was pleased to see Red walking, standing up and sitting down, without pain. After eating and chatting, he reminded me that Cole was coming over around seven.

Well-fed and relaxed, I felt more hopeful than I had in many years. But when the doorbell rang, my stomach flipped. Cole looked fit, his slender frame muscled out, his dark eyes smiling when he saw me. I grabbed him in a bear hug, tears threatening.

"Cole! Oh, my God. I thought you died."

Cole hugged me and stepped back. "You're the one who saved me. Luckily those V-C couldn't shoot a sitting target." He turned and showed me the scar across his head. "The bullet sliced my skull, but it barely touched my brain. God was watching."

I nodded, too emotional to speak. Red had warned me, but seeing Cole, listening to his voice, made it real. "I should've known your skull would be too thick," I finally joked.

He chuckled, his eyes as kind as ever. "Red said you had trouble remembering that night. It was truly FUBAR, and I was in and out. But I'll tell you what I saw, and you can fill in what you saw. Okay?"

I nodded. Fucked up beyond all repair was a very accurate portrayal of that night. I awaited his story, both terrified and curious.

Cole began. "I felt jumpy, couldn't get to sleep even after that long, scorching march. Ritz was up and about. That didn't worry me—just figured he felt restless too. But then he started messing with the wires." Cole chewed his lip. "That was his job, so I didn't think much of it. After that he headed to where Pee-wee was on guard. I guessed they might have something private going on and stayed away."

I frowned, not sure what Cole was getting at. "You think he cut the wires?"

"Yeah. It wasn't until later that it made any sense. I almost dozed off and woke with the explosions. I jumped up, grabbed my rifle, but a bullet hit my shoulder—knocked me down." Cole grimaced as if that memory stung.

"You crawled over and started digging in my wound. It hurt bad, and I panicked when I saw all the blood. Somehow you stopped the bleeding. I was praying for morphine when the V-C arrived." Cole stopped, his voice shaky. I put my hand on his arm, and he grabbed it, holding on.

"I'm real sorry 'bout the morphine. You would have died for sure if I hadn't fixed that bleeder. But when Charlie got the drop on me, I froze."

Cole relaxed. "All sins are forgiven when you save a life." He squeezed my hand and released it. I leaned back.

"They brought a kid for you to work on, and I was in and out. But then I made a big mistake—I moved. That's all I remember 'til I woke up on the ship."

I sighed, pleased that Cole's story confirmed my memories. "That's pretty much what I recall—except for Ritz. Did he survive?"

"He's MIA."

I frowned, puzzling on the implications.

"Was he angry at the time?" Red asked. "Do you remember?"

Cole shrugged. "He was a loner, so I didn't even notice."

"He never adjusted well," I said.

"Can you tell us what happened next?" Cole asked, his eyes on me.

I gathered up my courage and began. I explained that when they shot Cole, we were surrounded by a dozen or more gooks. Then a messenger arrived, and whatever he said caused such a commotion that my guard turned away. I took off, bullets whistling past me. But the Viet-Cong moved out—I thought to the west. I ran east across the camp until I found myself outside. Running back I tripped over Rog'.

"That's when I saw his throat cut." I shut up, head in my hands. I knew Red, Cole, and Rog' had been close friends, and we each took time out to manage our own grief. "I have trouble with what happened after that," I finally said.

"Did you hear about Pee-wee?" Cole asked.

I started to say no when a disgusting image overwhelmed my brain. I wanted to vomit, to run, to shield my eyes. Racing to the bathroom, I retched.

Red came and stood beside me. "Are you ill, or upset?"

I shook my head as words failed me. Cole joined Red. "Is this about Pee-wee?" When I stopped vomiting, they dragged me to the couch. I obediently sat but couldn't talk.

Heads turned as Laura left the bedroom and joined us. She squeezed in beside me. "You're okay, Pete. You're here in San Diego with your friends. You're very safe." As usual, her voice and touch calmed me. I looked up.

Red introduced Laura to Cole. "Anybody else want a beer?" He offered me a Coors. I accepted the bottle and sipped slowly.

Laura took a beer herself, staying on the couch. She turned to Cole. "Did Pee-wee die?"

It was clear she'd been listening the whole time.

Cole glanced from her to me and focused back on Laura. "Yeah, and the coroner's report is pretty gruesome." He stopped, watching me with worried eyes. "Maybe it'd go better if Pete told us what he knows."

"You up to that?" Red asked, touching my arm.

I shook my head. "I need to know what Cole learned."

Cole held my gaze, questioning, and I nodded. "Okay. The rest of our platoon found his body cut in pieces. Even the big brass were freaked out. The postmortem report said all the cuts were made by a machete."

"Same as Rog'?" Laura asked.

"Most likely, yeah."

I was grateful to Cole for telling that up front. Now I had words to fit my ugly memories. "I left Rog' and went to look for Pee-wee—found a foot. It shocked me so bad, I swore out loud. Next I found a hand, an arm, a leg. It felt like a bad dream, stumbling in the dark over pieces of a person—especially one I knew. At some point, I lost it."

"You see his head?" Cole asked, his eyes troubled.

As that image flashed before me, I found myself floating in the sky, looking down as if I were a disembodied spirit. Below me lay the camp, the Viet Cong, amid a bloody sea of human parts. Cole apologized, but it wasn't his fault. I knew for certain it was mine.

I heard Red and Laura talking but couldn't focus on their words. Laura took my hand, leading me into the bathroom. Closing the door, she stripped off all our clothes and guided me beneath the showerhead. The warm water soothed me. Wrapping us in towels, she led me into Red's bedroom and locked the door securely behind us.

Cuddled next to her, safe in her embrace, I sobbed until I fell asleep.

Chapter 23

The next morning I woke shortly after dawn. Red was off to classes, and Laura was already up, cleaning the apartment. After breakfast we caught a bus north to La Jolla Shores and hiked over to the beach. Five-foot waves rose and crashed in a soothing rhythm as we raced in the sand and dodged their frothy spray.

Laura didn't mention the previous night's discussion. Instead we chased seagulls and climbed cliffs, discovering a private, hidden cove. By noon, tired and hungry, we walked inland and ate tacos at a funky Mexican cantina. Relaxed and well fed, we rode the bus back home.

Red was there, changing clothes for work, and he glanced worriedly at me. But when he saw me smiling and at ease, he grinned.

"You guys have fun?"

"Yeah, thanks for loanin' out your bed."

Red chuckled. "Not the first time I've been kicked onto the couch."

I stared at the clock, calculating the time in Michigan. "Can I make a long-distance phone call?"

"Sure."

I walked into the bedroom and closed the door. Trusting my memory, I dialed Dr. Freedman and left him a message to call me back collect. While I was in the bedroom, Laura ran out for groceries. When she returned, I helped her make lasagna, chopped vegetables for salad, and buttered garlic bread while keeping an ear out for the phone.

It was late afternoon when Dr. Freedman called. I recognized his voice immediately and thanked him for calling, especially since we hadn't talked in years. He said he suspected my call might be important. I hoped he'd find that true.

"I'm out in San Diego. Cole is here! The guy who was bleedin' and the V-C shot again? He's alive. Last night I talked with him and Red, another friend, tryin' to figure out exactly what went down. But I freaked."

"What were you discussing at the time?"

I thought back. "Cole told us about Pee-wee, the other guy on guard, and how they found him cut in pieces. I remembered crawlin' in the dark, findin'… parts. That was gross. But it hit me so hard, I think there's somethin' more there, somethin' old."

Dr. Freedman was quiet, but I heard him turning pages and suspected he was reading through his notes. "That's how you first described your memory, 'parts and pieces,' which sounded rather odd at the time. In your childhood trauma, were there any 'parts and pieces'?"

I bit my lip and thought back, remembering how they broke the black man's fingers, the gun up to my head, the ugly man pushing my head down to his crotch. "I started vomitin' last night, like I did when that ugly guy made me suck his dick."

"Was this dead man's 'dick' one of those pieces?"

I almost gagged, but managed to croak, "Yes."

"How did you find it?"

I wanted to drop the phone and run. But I pictured Dr. Freedman, sitting in his chair puffing calmly on his pipe, and finally found the words. "His neck was severed, eyes removed, and penis stuck into his mouth." I gagged.

"I'd say that kill was very personal."

"I just found him—didn't kill him." My words rang defensive, even to my ears.

"I know that, Pete. But did you fantasize killing the man who abused you?"

"Yeah."

"Then be careful. Don't confuse your wishes with another person's act."

His words confused me, forcing me to slow down and think. But once I grasped their meaning, I felt as calm as the water in a forest pond, and I began to reason logically. I realized my rage, my lust to kill, had actually driven all the guilt. That guilt, in turn, caused me to deny my vengeful fantasies while putting my body in harm's way.

"It wasn't just the perp. Since I was ten years old, I've hated Pa."

"How did you handle that?"

"I ran. And lookin' back, I'd say that joinin' the Navy and movin' to Detroit were just two different types of runnin'. I had to run, or I'd have killed him." I wondered how many men I'd killed in his place.

"Did you ever hit your pa?"

"Once, when he broke my nose. Shortly after that, he had a heart attack, which still makes me feel guilty."

"Did you ever feel guilty before that?"

"All the time, and terrified too—afraid somethin' I did or said might trigger him again."

"Can you tell me what happened that night in Vietnam?"

My new mental clarity felt totally amazing, like a mood-enhancing drug. "When I discovered Pee-wee, I was already on extreme overload. I was livid about losin' Cole and Rog', terrified the V-C would capture me or kill me, and ashamed of both my rage and cowardice. But when I saw Pee-wee cut in pieces, I recalled he was a pervert and relived my old fantasy of tearing my abuser—and my pa—limb from limb. I guess the fear and guilt made me blank out."

"Do they know who killed him?"

"No. Since he was killed with a machete, we all assumed the murderer was Vietnamese, but there was this Marine, a peculiar guy named Ritz, and Cole saw him walkin' down that way."

"Is he alive?"

"He's MIA, so no one knows anythin' for sure." I sighed deeply as more pieces of my memory fell in place.

"Are you feeling any better?"

"Yeah. Thanks. I'll mail a check."

"You know, Pete, I'm very glad you called. I'd been thinking about you, praying that you were still okay."

"Thank you, Dr. Freedman. This time, I really think I am."

* * *

That evening Cole came back to Red's apartment. My talk with Dr. Freedman had brought up more memories, which I shared. I explained that while running through the camp, I passed all the guys who'd died in the explosions—some bodies full of shrapnel, some blown to bits, and a few with bullets in their heads. Since I feared the V-C were on my tail, I didn't stop to see if anyone was breathing. But from what I saw, no one survived.

"I think I understand why you chose to not remember," Cole said.

"Yeah," Red agreed. "You were all alone, escaping death or capture, falling over the bodies of dead friends. Any sane person would freak out. I'd say Pee-wee was just the final straw."

"You seem calmer tonight," Laura added, studying me.

I met her eyes, not ready to tell my friends about my shrink. Laura nodded.

We all shared theories on what happened, still unsure about what part Ritz had played. After several hours, it became crystal clear we needed facts. The next day, Laura and I went on a quest to the San Diego Naval Base office and requested a list of those KIA during April 1967.

A quick glance showed that every person in my squad, except for Cole, Ritz, and me, was killed that night. We asked for more information about Ritz.

"He remains MIA," the lady said. "So far no information, no POW reports, nothing found."

I told her I wanted to appeal my general discharge, and she gave me the required paperwork. At Red's place, Laura and I reviewed the forms.

"We need proof," I said. "Cole could write a statement, and I can write a statement, but I don't know if that will be enough." I sighed. "You think it's worth the effort?"

Laura pecked a kiss on the top of my head. "You deserve to be treated honorably."

I spent the afternoon writing up my memories. Then I called Cole and asked him to do the same. He brought his papers over the next day.

"I'm not much of a writer," Cole apologized. "But this is what I remember from that night."

Laura grabbed it first, nodding as she read. Then she started asking questions, clarifying facts. When she finished, she asked Cole, "Would you mind rewriting and adding more detail?"

"I see where you're going. It could be vital to know times, names, and locations in the camp."

Laura smiled. Studying what I'd written, she focused on details that confirmed my whereabouts, especially at the start, when the explosions and Rog' and Pee-wee's deaths were taking place.

"You'd make a good lawyer," Cole told her when we finished. "You're very logical, especially for a girl."

"Thanks—I think." She smiled wryly.

We flew home, and I mailed all the papers to the Navy, hoping they'd respond soon, hoping to show Pa that I wasn't such a screw-up. But the wheels of bureaucracy turned slowly, and for months I didn't hear a thing.

* * *

Our lives went back to their usual routines: school and work for me, Laura busy at her job. It was late February, early spring in Tennessee, when the letter from UCSD finally arrived. I would have waited for Laura, but I had to be at work. After holding the letter in my hand for several minutes, I took a deep breath and tore it open. The information hit me like a shockwave, and I called Laura's work, asking them to hunt her down.

She picked up the line. "Pete, what's wrong?"

"Nothin' at all. I just had to call and tell you. I got accepted!"

"At UCSD?"

"Yeah!"

She started laughing. "It's past time somebody recognized your talents. Does that mean we'll be moving?"

"Classes start in August, so no rush."

"Super! Let's go out and celebrate."

"I won't be home 'til after midnight."

"Oh, that's right."

She sighed, and I was happy that she missed me. "How about on Sunday?" I suggested.

"Sure. Love you, Pete."

"Love you too."

As soon as Laura hung up the phone, I started planning. We'd need money to move, money for an apartment, and money for tuition, books, and other supplies. The total was frightening. If Laura sold the farm, we'd be okay. Without that extra money, we'd both need to work full time just to support me starting school. My happy bubble burst, and work was waiting.

Chapter 24

I called Ma and said I'd been accepted into med school in La Jolla, a city just north of San Diego.

"California? You're moving out to California?" Her voice came close to tears. "Sarah and Bailey are leaving for Atlanta, and you want to move to California?"

I understood she wanted to be near us, wanted to share in any grandkids we might have. But for me there was a more immediate concern. I needed to make things right with Pa.

"We'll be over Sunday after church," I promised. "We can talk about it then."

When we arrived on Sunday, Ma was cooking up a feast. Laura immediately pitched in. She was fond of Ma, who'd filled a giant hole in Laura's life since the murder of her family. On our visits, Ma always took her aside, and they chatted as only women do. I left them to cook and gossip in the kitchen and went in search of Pa down by the creek.

The early spring flowers were in bloom, blanketing the banks of our creek in pastel rainbows. Was it really three years since Bruce led me through the gardens while pointing me along a different path? Wanting to thank him, to thank Jake, I stopped and said a prayer, praising Jesus for providing me with such gentle mentors.

Pa stood fishing, his attention focused on shadows in the water. I approached noisily to warn him. He turned, squinting until he saw my face.

"Hey, Pete."

"Catch anythin'?"

"Naw. They're bein' skittish."

I lowered myself onto a rock. "Ma tell you I've been accepted into med school?"

"Yep." He recast his line, dropping his bait by the far bank.

"I'll graduate this spring. You want to come?"

He grunted in irritation, staring at the creek. "How many degrees you think you need?"

"I'll be a doctor."

"What kinda doctor?"

"Not sure yet."

Pa reeled in his line, muttering, "Warn't catchin' nothin' no how." Climbing the bank, he sat beside me. "What you want?"

I sighed, already annoyed by his resistance. "I'd like to tell you a story, but you need to keep your mouth shut 'til I'm done."

His eyebrows rose. "This more nonsense about 'Nam?"

"Yep."

"You sure you want to tell me?"

"Yeah. You gonna listen?" I met his eyes, unflinching.

He frowned, hesitating, but curiosity won out. "Go ahead." He dropped his gaze to the water.

"It was a search-and-destroy mission, one platoon, travelin' light and fast up the coast, searchin' for a group of V-C raiders. We'd been out for two days, makin' time, and hadn't seen a thing—except for the scorched villages we passed. That night we set up camp, our squad to the south, the other squads to the north and east. We laid out our communications wire, wired some Claymores around the perimeter, and appointed two guys for each watch."

Pa lifted his gaze, drawn in by the familiar camp routines.

I explained how I woke with the explosions, grabbed my pack and rifle, and ran toward the fight. I saw Cole and stopped his bleeding. But when I turned around, I was looking down the barrel of an AK rifle.

Pa winced, and I knew I'd triggered him. "Need a break?" I asked.

"You're alive, so go on."

I nodded and continued. "Another gook brought a teenage boy, shot in the head. I couldn't really help him, but I did things to buy myself some time. By then, I could count a dozen V-C soldiers. No one else was movin' until Cole made a sound. The gooks shot him."

I grew quiet, and Pa asked, "What'd you do?"

"Nothin'. I was surrounded 'til a messenger arrived. Whatever he said distracted the V-C. So I ran. I ran past the tents damaged by explosions, past the mangled bodies of my squad, past the perimeter. Sneakin' back in the dark, I stumbled over Rog' and found his throat slit. Seein' that, I searched for Pee-wee."

I stopped and took a deep breath. Pa stayed silent.

"Cole told me he never got to sleep, and well before the explosions he saw Ritz, our communications expert, messin' with the wires and then walkin' off toward Pee-wee's post. Ritz is still MIA."

Pa's eyes widened.

Then I told him how the other squads moved in, finished off the gooks, and found me near Pee-wee—still in shock. "Since I couldn't remember and couldn't reason clearly, I didn't understand what they all must have thought. But no one seemed too sure about what happened, and when my memory didn't clear, when I couldn't do my work, they sent me home."

I watched Pa closely from the corner of my eye. He sat in silence, studying the water, mulling over everything I'd said. I gave him time.

Eventually he said, "What kind of person was this Ritz?"

"A loner: quiet, smart, not very social. He took anythin' you said real personal—defensive."

"What about Pee-wee?"

"Big guy, good soldier. I heard rumors he'd been accused of sodomy. I just figured he was gay and kept my distance. Maybe he did somethin' personal to Ritz, 'cause whoever killed him took the time to hack him up, cut off his limbs, head—other parts." Regretting I'd told him that, I hushed.

Pa scowled. "You saw that?"

"Crawlin' in the dark, I found the pieces. Freaked me out."

Pa took another breath, calming down. "But you were alive, so they blamed you."

"Until Cole told us about Ritz, no one knew different."

"You gonna tell the brass?"

"Already did, and Cole wrote down everythin' he saw."

"You got a hearin' scheduled?"

"Not yet."

Pa pursed his lips, and I stayed quiet. Eventually he said, "You're not a coward, Pete. I never should've said that."

I'd waited my whole life to hear those words, but now they seemed almost irrelevant. He'd called me a coward ever since I could remember, every time I cried, empathized with someone, or chose the less violent path. It flashed in my brain that I'd never been a coward. What I regretted were the times I'd lost my cool—behaved like him.

"Sorry I hit you," I said.

"I deserved it."

I raised my eyebrows in agreement. "You may not want to hear this, but I'll say it anyway. When I was a kid, I hated you, dreamed up ways to kill you, and that's what made me run. At eighteen, I ran off to join the Navy, three years later I ran off to Detroit, both times to protect *you* from *me*."

Pa's eyes grew dangerous. "You blame me?"

"No. Those were my emotions, in my head, but they drove me. Now I understand why I made those choices and why I blanked out that night in 'Nam."

Pa mulled over what I'd said, his brow furrowed. "You still hate me?"

"No." Surprisingly, I realized it was true. "Once I understood myself, I realized you and I are much the same."

He looked over, his expression turning puzzled when he saw the compassion in my eyes.

"I love you, Pa."

He drew and released a long, deep breath. "I always loved you, Pete—you're my son. And I'm beginnin' to think you might make a decent doctor."

* * *

After Ma's delicious dinner of savory pork chops with a tangy orange sauce, served with sweet potatoes and green beans she canned last fall, topped off by an apple cobbler with ice cream, Laura and I drove back to Knoxville. When I picked up the mail, I found a letter from the Navy. My eyes met Laura's as I slowly opened it. Taking out the folded form, I read:

> *To Pete Martin, HM3*
>
> *We reviewed your request for an upgrade in your discharge, and you presented key facts that were not previously known. Based on our review of all the evidence, we have scheduled a hearing to discuss this matter further. Please be present at the Naval Discharge Review Board in Washington DC at 1400 hours on Tuesday, April 4, 1972.*
>
> *Sincerely,*
> *Colonel Ace Seward, USMC*

I called Red and Cole and asked if they would join us at the hearing in D.C. Red wished me luck, although he couldn't come.

Cole agreed to meet us, wanting to support his testimony. Laura and I booked flights, and with those plans in place, I went back to school and work. But as the hearing date approached, I had trouble staying focused.

The morning of my hearing, Laura and I flew into D.C. and paid a cab to take us to the meeting. I felt as if I was going into battle when I entered the room and saw five distinguished officers waiting to pass judgment on my acts. Thank goodness Cole was there. I glanced at him, and he grinned back. The spokesman introduced himself as author of my letter, Colonel Seward.

"Corpsman Martin. We've received your written statement and that of Private First Class Martinez." He nodded at Cole, who must have introduced himself already. "Your accounts duplicate what we've previously known, except for Martinez' accusation of Lance-Corporal Ritz. As you know, Lance-Corporal Ritz is MIA. But that gave us a reason to review the evidence."

He went on to say that all the deaths in our squad were caused by V-C explosives, AK ammunition, and an unidentified machete. The machete could have come from either side, and without Ritz here, they couldn't be certain of his role, if any, in the slaughter. But the best part came next. He stated that everything they knew now absolved me of all wrongdoing and negligence of duty.

"In fact, your actions in saving Private Martinez aroused interest among our medical personnel. They were impressed by your ability, in the dark and under attack, to suture a torn artery. However, given the extra time required and the risk of infection, they decided that technique will not be taught to other corpsman."

Colonel Seward stopped, reaching underneath his desk. "Given that you served one year with the Marines, completed all the physical and educational requirements, and performed admirably under fire, I am honored to present you with this Fleet Marine Force Ribbon. Your discharge rank is now HM3 (FMF), and you are officially called 'Doc'."

Cole and Laura grinned, but my face was stiff with shock and a serious effort to contain my emotions. The colonel came down and handed me the ribbon. I saluted, and he saluted back.

"Your honorable discharge should arrive shortly. If you choose to re-enlist, we would be pleased to have you serve with us again." His face softened to a smile as he said, "You're dismissed."

I made it outside before the tears leaked down my cheeks. I hugged Laura, hiding my face in her hair.

Cole pounded on my back. "You did it, Pete, and you not only got an honorable discharge, you got a medal. May I see?"

I handed him my ribbon, drying my face as we waited for a taxi.

"We didn't even have a chance to argue," Laura said.

"You're disappointed?"

She laughed. "I was all prepared, so maybe just a little."

"They checked everything, the explosives and the bullets. Who'd have thought it?" Cole shook his head.

I shrugged. "It was a massacre. They had to learn what happened, try to prevent it ever happenin' again."

Chapter 24

Cole looked thoughtful. "You really think Ritz could murder Pee-wee? I mean Pee-wee had to be twice his size."

I rolled my eyes. "I'd guess Ritz offered sex, which got him close enough to kill. But that didn't satisfy his anger, so he chopped. When Rog' heard the commotion and came over, he got ambushed."

"You think Pee-wee did something sexual to Ritz?" Cole asked.

I nodded. "Sex abuse is disgustin' and shameful. It makes you so furious you want to commit murder. Dr. Freedman, my shrink back in Detroit, said that Pee-wee's death was very personal."

Cole's eyes asked a question he would never put in words.

I sighed, looking down. "That's why I freaked. When I was ten, this guy held me at gunpoint and forced me to do things I found totally disgustin'. Seeing Pee-wee's head made me relive that moment. I identified with his murderer."

I kept my eyes on the ground, too shamed to meet Cole's gaze.

Laura squeezed my hand. "It happens more often than you know. My boyfriend in high school confessed that his priest, of all people, made him do things. I was shocked and dumped him, thinking he was gay. Since then I've learned different. But it does make you want to shoot the bastard."

I relaxed, glancing warily at Cole.

He nodded, eyes steady. "What do you think became of Ritz?"

"He's probably dead. But if he's alive, I pity him."

Chapter 25

Back in Knoxville, Laura and I stepped off the plane into a soft April rain. We ransomed my car from the farthest parking lot and drove up the Alcoa Highway toward home.

"I've been thinkin'."

"About what?" She turned toward me.

"Our gettin' married. You want to get married?"

Laura wrinkled up her face and laughed. "That has to be the worst proposal ever."

"Well, that's just me. You can take me as I am—or not." I frowned, afraid I had insulted her and she might actually say no.

"Well I guess I could stay a while longer," she replied, green eyes twinkling.

"That's a pretty lukewarm yes."

We started giggling so hard I pulled off at Shoney's. Grabbing her in my arms, I held her as she snuggled close. "Will you marry me?" I asked, grinning at her happy face.

"Of course." She touched her lips to mine and sealed that promise.

We decided to get married at our family church in June, right before we left for San Diego. I invited Red, Cole, Lee, and Maria.

Of course all my family would be there. Laura invited two of her nursing friends along with Lou, Madge, and Anna from Detroit.

Over the next month, we heard from everyone but Anna. Cole and Red were flying in. Lou and Madge promised to drive down. Ma threw herself into planning food and flowers. She gave Laura her old wedding dress with permission to alter it any way she chose. Laura was delighted with the fabric, a heavy ivory silk covered with stitched pearls.

"This would cost a fortune now-a-days," Laura said, smoothing the dress between her hands. Searching in a sewing box, she pulled out shears and immediately started shaping it to fit. I'd never known her to sew, and it amazed me how easily she took on the project.

"You're good at that," I said.

"I've not had the time or money to make clothes, but my ma taught me to sew without a pattern, and to knit, crochet, and darn. I'm a dairy farmer's daughter after all."

"You churn butter?"

"No. But if you don't get your dirty feet off my wedding dress, I might churn your brain."

I moved my feet.

"Don't even watch. You're not supposed to see this dress until our wedding day."

I laughed. In our crowded apartment, that would be impossible. But watching all the time and care she put into that dress made me love her all the more.

Ma, Pa, Lee, Maria and Laura attended my college graduation. I felt silly in the cap and gown, but receiving the diploma made me proud. I even think Pa stood a little taller now that both his children had degrees.

With no more classes until fall, my forty-hour workweek seemed like a vacation. Laura and I went hiking in the mountains and swam at the old quarry outside Walnut Springs, sharing blankets and a lunch with Maria and Lee.

Laura and I set aside the time to sit down and discuss our money problems. With both of us working, we'd make enough to pay tuition. But during the last two years, the clinical rotations, I wouldn't have a single hour free.

"You could use the GI bill," Laura suggested.

I'd forgot. The U.S. Government would cover my tuition for the last couple years. With that worry off my shoulders, I felt hopeful.

A few days before the wedding, our guests began to trickle in. Mamaw and Aunt Kate made the trip from Nashville and were joined at the house by Lou and Madge. I had to laugh at Pa, surrounded by the ladies, but he seemed to enjoy all the attention.

Red and Cole arrived from San Diego, camping out in our overcrowded apartment. They teamed up with Lee to throw me a bachelor's party on the strip. It was fairly tame as bachelor parties go. But we drank more than we should, and Lee had a chance to meet my war buddies.

I wasn't sure how Lee would fit in, and at first he stayed quiet, listening to our stories. But when the subject turned to my discharge and appeal, Lee perked up his ears. "The Navy has a board just for that?"

"Your discharge determines what benefits you get," Cole said. "The GI Bill that pays for college? That only comes with an honorable discharge. Pete both needed and deserved it."

"There's a big difference between Military Law and Civil Law," Red explained. "Some lawyers study both and specialize in helping servicemen and veterans."

Lee's eyes lit up, and after a few drinks, he and Red were comparing legal aspects of the Korean versus the Vietnamese wars. As the evening progressed, I overheard Red and Lee picking information from each other's brains and knew they were destined to be friends.

Cole had a new job at the Navy shipyard doing underwater welding. It paid very well, and he enjoyed it—said the saltwater eased the weight of lifting and protected the shoulder that was injured back in 'Nam. I'd been worried he'd feel intimidated by all our schooling and degrees, but it didn't seem to faze him. Cole had both feet firmly planted on the ground and knew exactly who he was.

Our wedding day finally arrived. The church filled with flowers, and the food was all prepared. We were standing around waiting for the music to begin when a big black limo pulled into the parking lot. I gasped. Recalling the shoot-out in Detroit, my mind and body flipped to high alert.

"Go inside," I ordered Laura. "Tell Red and Cole *red alert*." Loosening the .45 from its ankle holster, I moved it to my pocket and approached the car.

As I advanced slowly—eyes fixed steady on the limo—I realized we had walked into a trap. My friends, family, and my precious bride were stuck in a building with one door. The best defense I could offer was just this—to come forward. If they took me, they might let the others go. I started praying.

The driver got out, a tall man in a suit, shoulder holster, and more firepower hidden in his clothes. He narrowed his eyes at me, focused on my pistol, and I stopped.

"Please holster your gun. I brought a friend," he said.

Pa stepped into view, his derringer pointed at the driver's head. "If you move, I'll kill you," he growled, holding his gun as still as steel.

I walked closer to the car, pistol ready, and yelled, "Come out, hands in the air!"

As the back door opened, I tensed and held my breath, but the body stepping out looked familiar. As he straightened up and grinned, my mouth gaped wide. Holstering my weapon, I hurried to the car and held out both my hands. He clasped them tight—even using his left hand.

"Lord help me." I stood staring.

"It's good to see you too, Tennessee." Observing my shock, Vic's eyes filled with concern. "You didn't check the morgue?"

I shook my head. Gradually recovering, I puzzled through his plan. "You planted your ID on someone else?"

He frowned and whispered, "Don't go there."

"Whose car?"

"FBI. I traded what's hidden in my head to stay alive."

"Oh!" I glanced at the driver, and he smiled. Pa had lowered his weapon and stepped back.

Vic's gaze moved behind me, and I spun, relaxing as Laura took my hand. Vic ogled Laura in her gown and grinned.

"Congratulations, Laura. You couldn't find a better man." He leaned down and kissed her on the cheek, adding in a whisper, "You look yummy in that dress."

Her eyes, wide with shock, remained on Vic. I sympathized with her surprise, but a surge of jealousy rushed through me as she feasted on his face, his winning smile. Had she chosen me because she thought Vic was dead?

I squeezed her hand. "Let's introduce Vic to all our friends."

But Laura didn't budge, eyes glued on him. My anger was rising when she spoke. "You heard about my parents?"

Vic bit his lip and took a deeper breath. "Laura, I'm so sorry. I never thought they'd go after you girls. Did you know they killed Anna?"

I put my arm around Laura as tears sprung to her eyes. To my surprise, Vic looked pretty close to crying. Had he been serious about Anna? As I studied the emotions he fought to contain, I recalled my own battles with guilt, rage, and grief, and my jealousy transformed into concern.

Laura took hold of both Vic's hands, her voice gentle. "I'm so sorry. We never heard a word about her death."

Vic took a deep breath, still struggling for control.

Laura gave him a moment to recover before adding, "I'm very glad you came. Since my parents can't be here, would you mind taking Dad's place and giving me away?"

Vic managed a smile. When he lifted his head to meet my eyes, I nodded. Given their history, it seemed appropriate. Then

Laura took my left hand, holding to Vic's right, and we three walked together toward the church.

As we approached, the wedding music started. My family and guests took their seats, and my friends in their suits paired up with Laura's bridesmaids, each dressed in a different pastel color, like spring flowers. As the guys and gals paraded up the aisle, ladies moving to the left, guys to the right, I joined my friends and turned around to watch.

Laura looked like a princess in her hand-sewn dress, silk and pearls shimmering in the sun. The organist switched to the formal wedding march, and Vic led Laura up the aisle, placing her hand carefully in mine. The minister spoke briefly, we each said our vows, and I slipped a gold ring onto her finger. She held my hand tight as she slipped the ring on mine. I couldn't take my eyes off her face, and when she returned my kiss, I felt blessed.

Ma served a picnic dinner: fried chicken with potatoes, country gravy, biscuits that melted in your mouth, and apple pie à la mode. I introduced Vic to my very curious friends, although he didn't say much. After almost an hour, he pulled me away.

Walking toward the car, Vic dropped his voice to a whisper. "Sorry 'bout the money. The Feds get real fussy about funds. In order to qualify, I had to hand over all my 'illicitly gained' profits."

I shrugged. "Once it was gone, I didn't miss it. I got what I wanted." I grinned, nodding at Laura with her friends.

Vic followed my gaze. "You did well."

I recalled the FBI detective and his questions. "Did you ask the Feds to put me under surveillance?"

"Yeah, why? Did something happen?"

"When I drove north to pick up Laura, they stopped and questioned me."

"Sorry. I thought the Mafia would go for you guys first—not the girls."

"Did you tell the Feds about Angel?"

"Definitely." Vic grimaced.

"Thanks." I put a hand on his arm, seeing that memory still hurt him. "What happens to you now?"

He frowned and dug his toe into the grass. "I'll prepare to be a witness while doing my best to stay alive."

"Good choice. How's your hand?"

"Better. The Feds found me a surgeon in Ann Arbor, and he grafted a couple broken bones. Now I can use it, and it's slowly getting stronger." I watched his face as he clenched his fist and opened his hand straight. He never even winced, which made me smile.

"Were you able to get clean?"

"Pretty much." He shrugged and dropped his gaze.

Vic's answer worried me, but it wasn't the time or place for that discussion. "Are we still at risk?"

"Possibly, but they're putting those assholes behind bars as we speak. If I can keep them there, we'll all be safe."

"Thanks so much for comin'. I'll sleep much better knowin' you're alive."

Vic raised his eyes, forehead wrinkled in concern. "I hate that I caused you more grief. How's the sleep?"

"Okay. Between my shrink and my friends, not to mention Laura, I've been able to remember and move forward. I'm headed off to medical school next."

"So I heard. Congrats." His expression remained kind but terribly sad.

"How long will you be in the program?"

He sighed. "I have to make it through the trials. Another five years if I'm lucky. But if those guys walk, it could be life."

Vic's sadness scared me. "I'll be in La Jolla at the UCSD med school. If they'll let you call, we can talk—anytime."

After glancing at his driver, who pointed to his watch, Vic reached over and took hold of my hands. "I have to go. I don't know when I'll see you, don't know if I can call, but I definitely plan to stay alive. You do the same, and take good care of Laura."

"Wait!" I ran to my car and pulled my sketchpad from the seat, finding and tearing out a sheet. I hurried back and handed it to Vic.

He stared. "My God, it's Anna." His eyes filled with tears as he bit hard on his lip. "Thank you. This is priceless."

"Take care of yourself, Vic."

"Until whenever, Tennessee." He grabbed my shoulders, hugging me hard, and turned abruptly toward the car. Laura came over as the limo roared away, churning up a cloud of memories.

Chapter 26

Over the next few days, Laura and I said farewell to our guests. A week later, with all our belongings stuffed inside, we squeezed into my Beetle and said our thank-yous and goodbyes to Maria and Lee. They promised to come visit before the year was through.

The first day out, we drove to Little Rock. In a dingy motel beside the interstate, we made love all night long. Getting up lazy and late the next morning, we breakfasted on snack bars and drove straight west to Kansas. I'd thought Ohio and Michigan were flat, but I'd never been on the Great Plains. We watched for hours as a giant black thunderhead approached from the west. Somewhere near Salina, it attacked, hammering with hail and buffeting my little car with violent gusts of wind. I pulled off at a diner, although that didn't offer much protection.

The storm passed quickly, the skies cleared, and the stars lay thick across the Milky Way. The night looked so beautiful, the weather felt so mild, I turned onto a dirt road and drove out into the grasslands. Opening my sleeping bag double in a field, we lay on our backs and stared at stars so brilliant they lit up the night sky. We made love beneath the watchful stars and slept.

The next day I felt different, as if all the tension in my body had poured out. I couldn't recall when I'd relaxed so completely. On the ship, we had emergencies 24/7, and life in Vietnam was filled with death. In Detroit, between the riots, the drug trade, and the cops, I never knew when somebody might kill me. Even working at Eastern State, I had to watch my back. I couldn't remember ever feeling quite this safe, even as a little kid.

I'd never met anybody quite like Laura. She wanted to visit every park and attraction and approached each new place with the wide-eyed excitement of a child. We made a lot of side trips to see state parks, lakes, buffalo, and even wild horses. I sketched her in all those different settings as she smiled more, talked more, and laughed. I realized Laura, like me, was unwinding, feeling safe.

When we finally got to Denver, I splurged for a hotel. In luxury we showered, shampooed, and dressed for supper. I told Laura this was our first date, and we joked throughout the meal, pretending that was true. After making love on the silky soft sheets, she fell asleep, and I lay there admiring the curves of her sleek body as rays of silvery moonlight stole across the room.

The next day we meandered over mountains and up canyons, stopping to hike, pick bouquets of wildflowers, and soak our feet in frigid mountain streams. Colorado exceeded all my expectations. I was ready to stop and put down roots. Nightfall found us in Montrose, a small town at the southern edge of the Grand Mesa.

The next morning we drove to the Black Canyon, a state park Laura had seen advertised. We followed the signs and tracked slowly down a dirt road, traveling straight across the mesa. The land appeared flat, covered with sagebrush and mesquite, populated only with lizards, snakes, and rodents.

After an hour, I began to worry. "Did we miss it?"

"There haven't been any signs for miles," Laura said.

"You want to turn around? I think we're lost."

"I know exactly where we are—the canyon's lost." Laura's green eyes sparkled, filled with merriment.

"Well then, let's go a little farther." I picked up speed, and we bumped along the road until it curved sharply, ending in a parking lot. The asphalt looked strangely out of place.

"I think we're here," I said, hoping we hadn't come this far for nothing. We parked and walked across the pavement to a railing. Gasping in unison, we both grabbed at the rail.

In front of us, the sky dropped straight down almost a mile, the canyon barely two hundred feet across. The sides were black rock, eroded into crags, which housed the eagles circling below. And at the very bottom, a wiggly ribbon of bright green marked the path of the Gunnison. Gazing deep into this ancient scar, I found a path—not downward between the jagged cliffs—but upward from my hellish past into a hopeful future.

"Unreal!" I turned to Laura, wanting to explain, but words couldn't capture what I felt.

"It's awe inspiring," she whispered, "almost as though I'm in heaven looking down."

"Maybe we are." Grabbing Laura in my arms, I swung her in the air, laughing as she screamed and clung to me. I spun her 'round, and 'round while throwing my past sins to the wind and soaring like an eagle off the cliff.

Thanks to Dr. Freedman, I'd forgiven myself and all the other sinners in my life. Thanks to Lee, Red, and Cole, I had a future. And thanks to Vic, I wouldn't spend that future on the run. Despite the agonies I'd suffered getting here, the prize I'd taken home—the one I held tight in my arms—was worth every sleepless night and every anguished hour, through all the years we'd have the grace to share.

Thank you, Lord.